THE PATIENCE OF THE SPIDER

ANDREA CAMILLERI

THE PATIENCE OF THE SPIDER

Translated by Stephen Sartarelli

PICADOR

First published 2007 by Penguin Books,
a member of Penguin Group (USA) Inc., New York

First published in Great Britain 2007 by Picador

This edition published in Great Britain 2008 by Picador
an imprint of Pan Macmillan Ltd
Pan Macmillan, 20 New Wharf Road, London N1 9RR
Basingstoke and Oxford
Associated companies throughout the world
www.panmacmillan.com

ISBN 978-0-330-44223-7

3 5 7 9 8 6 4 2

A CIP catalogue record for this book is available from
the British Library.

Typeset by SetSystems Ltd, Saffron Walden, Essex
Printed and bound in Great Britain by
Mackays of Chatham plc, Chatham, Kent

Visit **www.picador.com** to read more about all our books
and to buy them. You will also find features, author interviews and
news of any author events, and you can sign up for e-newsletters
so that you're always first to hear about our new releases.

THE PATIENCE OF THE SPIDER

ONE

He jolted awake, sweaty and short of breath. For a few seconds he didn't know where he was. Then the soft, regular breathing of Livia, who lay asleep beside him, brought him back to a familiar, reassuring reality. He was in his bedroom in Marinella. What had yanked him from his sleep was a sharp pang, cold as a knife blade, in his wounded shoulder. He didn't need to look at the clock on the nightstand to know that it was three-thirty in the morning – actually, three twenty-seven and forty seconds. The same thing had been happening to him for the last twenty days, ever since the night Jamil Zarzis, a trafficker in small Third World children, had shot and wounded him, and he had reacted by killing the man. Twenty days, but it was as though the mechanism of time had got stuck at that moment. Some gear in the part of his brain that measures the passing hours and days had gone '*clack*', and ever since, if he was asleep, he would wake up, and if he was awake, everything around him would stop in a sort of imperceptible freeze-frame. He knew very well that during that split-second duel, it had never crossed his mind to check what time it was, and yet – and this he remembered very clearly – the moment the bullet fired by Jamil Zarzis penetrated his flesh, a voice inside him – an impersonal female voice, slightly metallic, like the voices you hear over PA systems in train stations and supermarkets – had said, 'It is three twenty-seven and forty seconds.'

*

'Were you with the inspector?'

'Yes, Doctor.'

'Your name?'

'Fazio, Doctor.'

'How long has he been wounded?'

'Well, Doctor, the exchange of fire took place around three-thirty. So, a little more than half an hour ago. Oh, Doctor...'

'Yes?'

'Is it serious?'

The inspector was lying down, utterly still, eyes shut, which led everyone to think he was unconscious and they could speak openly. Whereas in fact he heard and understood everything. He felt simultaneously dazed and lucid, but had no desire to open his mouth and answer the doctor's questions himself. Apparently the injections they'd given him to kill the pain had affected his whole body.

'Don't be silly! All we have to do is extract the bullet lodged in his shoulder.'

'O Madonna santa!'

'There's no need to get so upset! It's a piece of cake. Besides, I really don't think it did much damage. With a bit of physical therapy, he should recover one hundred per cent use of his arm. But why, may I ask, are you still so concerned?'

'Well, you see, Doctor, a few days ago the inspector went out by himself on an investigation . . .'

✻

Now, as then, he keeps his eyes closed. But he can no longer hear the words, which are drowned out by the loud, pounding surf. It must be windy outside, the whole shutter is vibrating from the force of the gusts, emitting a kind of wail. It's a good thing he's still convalescing; he can stay under the covers for as long as he wants. Consoled by this thought, he decides to open his eyes just a crack.

✻

Why could he no longer hear Fazio talking? He opened his eyes just a crack. The two men had stepped a short distance away from the bed and were over by the window. Fazio was talking and the doctor, dressed in a white smock, was listening, a grave expression on his face. Suddenly Montalbano realized he had no need to hear Fazio's words to know what he was saying to the doctor. Fazio, his friend, his trusty right-hand man, was betraying him. Like Judas. He was obviously telling the doctor about the time he'd found the inspector lying on the beach, drained of strength after the terrible chest pain he'd had in the water . . . Imagine the doctors' reaction upon hearing this wonderful news! Before ever removing that damned bullet, they would give him

the works: examine him inside and out, poke him full of holes, lift up
his skin piece by piece to see what there was underneath . . .

*

His bedroom is the same as it's always been. No, that's not true. It's different, but still the same. Different because there are Livia's things on the dresser: purse, hairpins, two little perfume bottles. And, on the chair across the room, a blouse and skirt. And though he can't see them, he knows there's a pair of pink slippers somewhere near the bed. He feels a surge of emotion. He melts, goes all soft inside, turns to liquid. For twenty days this has been his new refrain, and he doesn't know how to put a stop to it. The slightest thing will set it off and bring him, treacherously, to the point of tears. He's embarrassed, ashamed of his new emotional fragility, and has to create elaborate defences to prevent others from noticing. But not with Livia. With her he couldn't pull it off. So she decided to help him, to lend him a hand by dealing firmly with him, not allowing him any opportunities to let himself go. But it's no use. Because this loving approach on Livia's part also triggers a mixed emotion of happiness and sadness. He's happy that Livia used up all her holiday to come and look after him, and he knows that the house is happy to have her there. Ever since she arrived, when he looks at his bedroom in sunlight it seems to have its colour back, as though the walls had been repainted a luminous white.

Since nobody can see him, he wipes away a tear with a corner of the sheet.

*

White all around, and amidst the white, only the brown of his naked skin. (Was it once pink? How many centuries ago?) A white room, in which he's being given an electrocardiogram. The doctor studies the long strip of paper, shakes his head in doubt. Terrified, Montalbano imagines that the graph the doctor is examining looks exactly like the seismograph of the Messina earthquake of 1908, which he once saw reproduced in a history magazine: a crazy, hopeless jumble of lines traced as if by a hand driven mad by fear.

They've found me out! *he thinks to himself.* They realize that my heart functions on alternating current, higgledy-piggledy, and that I've had at least three heart attacks!

Then another doctor, also in a white smock, enters the room. He looks at the strip, at Montalbano, and at his colleague.

'Let's do it again,' he says.

Maybe they can't believe their eyes, can't understand how a man with an electrocardiogram like that is still in a hospital bed and not on a marble slab in the morgue. They look at the new strip, their heads now very close together.

'Let's do a telecardiogram,' is the verdict. The doctors seem perplexed.

Montalbano wishes he could tell them that, if this is the way it is, they shouldn't even bother extracting the bullet. They should let him die in peace. But, damn it, he forgot to make a will. The house in

Marinella, for example, should definitely go to Livia, so that some fourth cousin doesn't turn up and claim it.

✳

Right, because the house in Marinella has been his for a few years now. He never thought he'd be able to buy it. It cost too much for the salary he earned, which barely let him set anything aside. Then one day his father's former partner wrote to him saying he was ready to liquidate his father's share of the vineyard, which amounted to a considerable sum. So not only had he the money to buy the house, but there was a fair amount left over to put away. For his old age. And that was why he needed to draw up a will, since, without wanting to, he'd become a man with property. Once again, however, after he got out of the hospital he couldn't bring himself to go and see the notary. But if he ever did get around to seeing him, the house would go to Livia, that much was certain. As for François, the son who wasn't his son but could have been, he knew exactly what to leave him. Enough money to buy himself a nice car. He could already see the indignant expression on Livia's face. What? And spoil him like that? Yes, ma'am. A son who wasn't a son but could (should?) have been one should be spoiled much more than a son who's really a son. Twisted logic, yes, but still logical. And what about Catarella? Surely he had to put Catarella in his will. So what would he leave him? Certainly not any books. He tried to recall an old song of the Alpine Regiment called 'The Captain's Testament' or something similar, but couldn't remember it. The watch! That was it. He would leave Catarella his father's watch, which his business partner had sent to him. That way he could feel like part of the family. The watch was the answer.

*

He can't read the clock on the wall in the cardiology unit because there is a kind of greyish veil over his eyes. The two doctors are very attentively watching some sort of TV screen, occasionally moving a mouse.

One of them, the doctor who's supposed to perform the operation, is named Strazzera, Amedeo Strazzera. This time the machine spits out not a strip of paper but a series of photographs or something similar. The two doctors study and study them, then finally sigh as though worn out after a long walk. Strazzera approaches while his colleague goes and sits down in a chair — white, of course. The doctor looks sternly at the inspector and bends forward. Montalbano is expecting him to say:

'You must stop pretending you're alive! Shame on you!'

How does the poem go?

'The poor man, not knowing how much he'd bled, / kept on fighting when in fact he was dead.'

But the doctor says nothing and begins to sound his chest with the stethoscope. As if he hasn't already done this at least twenty times. Finally he straightens back up, looks over at his colleague, and asks:

'What do we do?'

'I would let Di Bartolo have a look at him,' says the other.

Di Bartolo! A legend. Montalbano had met him a while back. By now he must be over seventy. A skinny old man with a little white beard that made him look like a goat, he could no longer conform to human society or the rules of common courtesy. Once, after examining, in a manner of speaking, a man known to be a ruthless loan shark, he told the patient he couldn't tell him anything because he was unable to locate his heart. Another time, in a cafe, he said to a man he'd never seen before, who was sipping a coffee, 'Do you know you're about to have a heart attack?' And lo and behold, he had a heart attack right then and there, maybe because a luminary such as Di Bartolo had just told him it was coming.

But why do these two want to call in Di Bartolo if there is nothing more to be done? Maybe they want to show the old master what a phenomenon this Montalbano is, the way he inexplicably goes on living with a heart that looks like Dresden after the bombing.

While waiting, they decide to take him back to his room. As they're opening the door to push the stretcher through, he hears Livia's voice call out desperately:

'Salvo! Salvo!'

He doesn't feel like answering. Poor thing! She'd come down to Vigàta to spend a few days with him and got this nice surprise instead.

*

'What a nice surprise!' Livia had said to him the day before, when, upon his return from a check-up at Monte-lusa Hospital, he'd appeared in the doorway with a large bouquet of roses in his hands. And she'd burst into tears.

'Come on, don't start!' he'd said, barely holding back himself.

'Why shouldn't I?'

'Well, you never have before!'

'And when have you ever given me a bouquet of roses before?'

He lays his hand on her hip, but gently, so as not to wake her.

*

He'd forgotten — or else hadn't noticed during his earlier meetings with him — that Dr Di Bartolo not only looked but also sounded like a goat.

'Good day, everybody,' he bleats upon entering, followed by ten or so doctors, all dressed without fail in white smocks and crowding into the room.

'Good day,' replies everybody — that is, Montalbano, since he's the only body in the room when the doctor appears.

Di Bartolo approaches the bed and looks at him with interest.

'I'm glad to see that, despite my colleagues' efforts, you can still understand and know what you want.'

He makes a gesture and Strazzera appears beside him and hands him the test results. Di Bartolo barely glances at the first sheet and then tosses it onto the bed, does the same with the second, ditto the third and the fourth. In a matter of seconds, Montalbano's head and torso disappear under the paper. In the end he hears the doctor's voice but can't see him because the photos of the telecardiogram are over his eyes.

'Mind telling me why you called me here?'

The bleat sounds rather irritated. Apparently the goat is getting cross.

'Well, Doctor,' Strazzera's voice hesitantly begins, 'the fact is, one of the inspector's men told us that a few days ago he'd had a serious episode of...'

Of what? Montalbano can no longer hear Strazzera. Maybe he's telling the next instalment in Di Bartolo's ear. Instalment? This isn't some soap opera. Strazzera said 'episode'. But isn't a soap opera instalment called an episode?

'Pull him up for me,' orders Dr Di Bartolo.

They remove the sheets of paper covering him and gently lift him up. A circle of doctors in white surround the bed, religiously silent. Di Bartolo applies the stethoscope to Montalbano's chest, moves it an inch, then moves it another inch and stops. Seeing his face so close, the inspector notices that the doctor's jaws are moving continuously, as if he is chewing gum. All at once, he understands. The doctor is ruminating. Dr Di Bartolo actually is a goat. Who now hasn't moved for a long time. He's listening, immobile. What do his ears hear in there? Montalbano wonders. Buildings collapsing? Fissures suddenly opening up? Subterranean rumbles? Di Bartolo keeps listening interminably, not moving a fraction of an inch from the spot he's singled out. Doesn't it hurt his back to stay bent over like that? The inspector begins to sweat from fear. The doctor straightens up.

'That's enough.'

The other doctors set Montalbano back down.

'In my opinion,' the luminary concludes, 'you could shoot him another three or four times, extract the bullets without anaesthesia, and his heart would definitely stand up to it.'

Then he leaves, without saying goodbye to anyone.

Ten minutes later, the inspector's in the operating room. There's a bright white light. A man stands over him, holding a kind of mask in his hand, which he places over Montalbano's face.

'Breathe deeply,' he says.

He obeys. And can't remember anything else.

✳

How is it, he asks himself, *they haven't yet invented an aerosol cartridge for when you can't sleep? Something you stick in your nose and push, and the gas or whatever it is comes out, and you fall asleep right away?*

That would be handy, an anti-insomnia anaesthesia. He suddenly feels thirsty, gets out of bed gingerly, to avoid waking Livia, goes into the kitchen, and pours himself a glass of mineral water from an already open bottle. Now what? He decides to exercise his right arm a little, the way the physiotherapist taught him. One, two, three, and four. One, two, three, and four. The arm works fine. Well enough for him to drive with ease.

Strazzera was absolutely right. Except that sometimes his arm falls asleep, the way your leg does when you stay in the same position for too long without moving and the whole limb feels full of pins and needles. Or armies of ants. He drinks another glass of water and goes back to bed. Feeling him slip under the covers, Livia murmurs something and turns her back to him.

*

'Water,' he implores, opening his eyes.

Livia pours him a glass, holding his head up with her hand at the base of the skull so he can drink. Then she puts the glass back on the nightstand and disappears from the inspector's field of vision. He manages to sit up a little in bed. Livia's standing in front of the window, and Dr Strazzera is beside her, talking to her at great length. Montalbano hears a little giggle come from Livia. What a witty guy, this Dr Strazzera! And why is he hanging all over Livia? And why doesn't she feel the need to take a step back? OK, I'll show them.

'Water!' he yells in rage.

Livia jumps, startled.

'Why is he drinking so much?' Livia asks.

'It must be an effect of the anaesthetic,' says Strazzera. And he adds: 'But, you know, Livia, the operation was child's play. I was even able to make it so that the scar will be practically invisible.'

Livia gives the doctor a grateful smile, which infuriates the inspector even more.

An invisible scar! So he won't have any problem entering the next Mr Muscle competition.

*

Speaking of muscle, or whatever you want to call it . . . He slides over, ever so gently, until his body is pressed up against Livia's back. She seems to appreciate the contact, to judge by the way she moans in her sleep.

Montalbano extends a cupped hand and places it over one of her tits. As if by conditioned reflex, Livia puts her hand over his. But here the operation grinds to a halt. Because Montalbano knows perfectly well that if he proceeds any further, Livia will put an immediate stop to it. It's already happened once, on his first night back from the hospital.

'No, Salvo. Out of the question. I'm afraid you might hurt yourself.'

'Come on, Livia. It's my shoulder that was injured, not my—'

'Don't be vulgar. Don't you understand? I wouldn't feel comfortable, I'd be afraid to . . .'

But his muscle, or whatever you want to call it, doesn't understand these fears. It has no brain, is not used to thinking. It refuses to listen to reason. So it just stays there, bloated with rage and desire.

✳

Fear. Terror. He begins to feel this the second day after the operation, when, around nine in the morning, the wound starts to throb painfully. Why does it hurt so much? Did they forget a piece of gauze in there, as so often happens? Or maybe not gauze, but a thirty-centimetre scalpel? Livia notices at once and calls Strazzera. Who comes running, probably leaving in the middle of some open-heart surgery. But that's how things are now: the moment Livia calls, Strazzera comes running.

The doctor says the reaction was to be expected, there's no reason for Livia to be alarmed. And he sticks another needle into Montalbano. Less than ten minutes later, two things happen: first, the pain starts to subside; and second, Livia says:

'The commissioner's here.'

And she leaves. Bonetti-Alderighi enters the room accompanied by the chief of his cabinet, Dr Lattes, whose hands are folded in prayer, as if he were at a dying man's bedside.

'How are you? How are you?' asks the commissioner.

'How are you? How are you?' Lattes echoes him, as in a litany.

The commissioner begins to speak, but Montalbano hears only scraps of what he's saying, as if a strong wind were carrying away his words.

'... and therefore I've recommended you be given a solemn citation ...'

'... solemn citation ...' echoes Lattes.

'La-de-da-de-da-de-ation,' says a voice in Montalbano's head. Wind.

'... while awaiting your return, Inspector Augello ...'

'Oh good fellow, good fellow,' says the same voice in his head. Wind.

Eyelids drooping, inexorably closing.

*

Now his eyelids are drooping. Maybe he can finally fall asleep. Just like this, pressed up against Livia's warm body. But there's that damn shutter that keeps wailing with every gust of wind.

What to do? Open the window and try to close the shutter more tightly? Not a chance. It would surely wake Livia up. But maybe there is a solution. No harm in trying. Instead of fighting the shutter's wail, try to echo it, incorporate it in the rhythm of his own breathing.

'Iiiih!' goes the shutter.

'Iiiih!' goes the inspector, softly, lips barely open.

'Eeeeh!' goes the shutter.

'Eeeeh!' echoes the inspector.

That time, however, he didn't keep his voice down. In a flash, Livia opens her eyes and sits up in bed.

'Salvo! Are you unwell?'

'Why?'

'You were moaning!'

'I must have been doing it in my sleep. Sorry. Go back to sleep.'

Damned window!

TWO

A gelid blast is blowing in through the wide-open window. It's always that way in hospitals. They cure your appendicitis and then make you die of pneumonia. He's sitting in an armchair. Only two days left, and he can finally go back to Marinella. But since six o'clock that morning, squads of women have been cleaning everything: corridors, rooms, cupboards, windows, doorknobs, beds, chairs. It's as if a great cloud of clean-up mania has descended on the place. Sheets, pillowcases, blankets are changed, the bathroom sparkles so brightly it's blinding; you need sunglasses to go in there.

'What's going on?' he asks a nurse who's come to help him get back in bed.

'Some big cheese is coming.'

'Who?'

'I don't know.'

'Listen, couldn't I just stay in the armchair?'

'No, you can't.'

A little while later, Strazzera turns up, disappointed not to find Livia in the room.

'I think she might drop in later,' Montalbano sets his mind at rest.

But he's just being mean. He said 'might' just to keep the doctor on tenterhooks. Livia assured him she'd be there to see him, only a little late.

'So who's coming?'

'Petrotto. The undersecretary.'

'What for?'

'To congratulate you.'

Fuck. That's all he needs. The honourable Gianfranco Petrotto, former chamber deputy, now undersecretary of the interior, though once convicted for corruption, another time for graft, and a third time let off the hook by the statute of limitations. An ex-Communist and ex-Socialist, now a triumphant member of the party in power.

'Couldn't you give me an injection to knock me out for three hours or so?' he implores Strazzera.

The doctor throws his hands up and goes out.

The honourable Gianfranco Petrotto arrives, preceded by a powerful roar of applause that echoes through the corridor. But the only people allowed to enter the room with him are the prefect, the commissioner, the hospital superintendent, and a deputy from the politico's retinue.

'Everyone else, wait outside!' he commands with a shout.

Then his mouth opens and closes, and he begins to talk. And talk. And talk. He doesn't know that Montalbano has plugged his ears with surgical cotton to the point where they feel like they're about to explode and can't hear the bullshit he's saying.

✻

19

It's been a while now since the shutter stopped wailing. He barely has time to look at the clock – four forty-five – before he falls asleep at last.

*

In his sleep he could faintly hear the telephone ringing and ringing.

He opened one eye, looked at the clock. Six o'clock. He'd slept barely an hour and fifteen minutes. He got up in a hurry, wanting to stop the ringing before it reached Livia in the depths of her sleep. He picked up the receiver.

'Chief, whadd I do, wake you up?'

'Cat, it's six in the morning. On the dot.'

'Actually my watch gots six oh tree.'

'That means it's a little fast.'

'You sure 'bout that, Chief?'

'Absolutely.'

'OK, so I'll put it tree minutes slow. Tanks, Chief.'

'You're welcome.'

Catarella hung up. Montalbano did likewise, then headed back to the bedroom. Halfway there, he started cursing. What kind of damn phone call was that? Catarella calls him at the crack of dawn to find out if his watch has the right time? At that moment the phone rang again. The inspector quickly picked up the receiver after the first ring.

'Beck y'pardin, Chief, but that bizniss 'bout the time made me forget to tell you the real reason for the phone call I jes phoned you about.'

'So tell me.'

'Seems some girl's motorbike's been seized.'

'Seized or robbed?'

'Seized.'

Montalbano fumed. But he had no choice but to smother his urge to yell.

'And you wake me up at six in the morning to tell me the Carabinieri or Customs police have impounded a motorbike? To tell *me*? Pardon my French, but I don't give a fuck!'

'Chief, you kin speak whichever langwitch ya like wittout beckin my pardin, though, beckin y'pardin, it sounds a lot to me like a 'talian,' Catarella said respectfully.

'And furthermore, I'm not on duty, I'm still convalescing!'

'I know, Chief, but it wasn't neither the Customs or the Canabirreri that had the seizure.'

'Well, then who was it?'

' 'Ass just it, Chief. Nobody knows. Ann'ass why they tol' me to call you poissonally in poisson.'

'Listen, is Fazio there?'

'No, sir, he's at the scene.'

'How about Inspector Augello?'

'Him too.'

'So who's left there at the station?'

'For the moment, Chief, 's jes me holdin' down the fort. Mr Inspector Augello axed me to do 'is doody for 'im, so 'ass what I'm doin'.'

Good God! A danger to be avoided as quickly as possible. Catarella was capable of triggering a nuclear war with a simple purse-snatching. But was it possible Fazio and Augello would go to all this trouble for a routine seizure of a motorbike? And why did they have Catarella call him?

'Listen, I want you to do something. Get ahold of Fazio and tell him to phone me at once here in Marinella.'

He hung up.

'What is this, Termini Station?' said a voice behind him.

He turned around. It was Livia, eyes flashing with anger. When she'd got up she'd slipped on Montalbano's shirt from the day before instead of her dressing gown. Seeing her thus attired, the inspector felt an overwhelming desire to embrace her. But he held himself back, knowing that Fazio would be calling at any moment.

'Livia, please, my job . . .'

'You should do your job at the station. And only when you're on active duty.'

'You're right, Livia. Now come on, go back to bed.'

'Bed? I'm awake now, thanks to you! I'm going to go and make some coffee,' she said.

The telephone rang.

'Fazio, would you be so kind as to tell me what the fuck is going on?' Montalbano asked in a loud voice, since there was no longer any need for precaution. Livia was not only awake, but pissed off.

'Stop using obscenities!' Livia screamed from the kitchen.

'Didn't Catarella tell you?'

'Catarella didn't tell me a damn thing—'

'Are you going to stop or not?' yelled Livia.

'—all he told me was something about a motorbike being seized, but not by the Carabinieri or the Customs police. Why the fuck—'

'Knock it off, I said!'

'—are you guys bothering me with this stuff? Go and see if it was the traffic police!'

'No, Chief. If anything was seized, it was the girl who owned the motorbike.'

'I don't understand.'

'There's been a kidnapping, Chief.'

A kidnapping? In Vigàta?

'Tell me where you are and I'll come right over,' he said without thinking.

'Chief, it's too complicated to find your way out here. If it's all right with you, a squad car'll be at your place in about an hour. That way you won't have to tire yourself out by driving.'

'OK.'

He went into the kitchen. Livia had put the coffeepot on the ring and was now spreading the tablecloth over the small kitchen table. To smooth it out, she had to bend all the way forward, so that the inspector's shirt she was wearing became too short.

Montalbano couldn't restrain himself. He took two steps forward and embraced her tightly from behind.

'What's got into you?' Livia asked. 'Come on, let go! What are you trying to do?'

'Guess.'

'You might hurt yo—'

The coffee rose in the pot. Nobody turned off the flame. The coffee burned. The flame remained lit. The coffee started boiling. Nobody bothered with it. The coffee spilled out of the pot, extinguishing the flame on the ring. The gas continued to flow.

'Doesn't it smell strangely of gas?' Livia asked languidly a bit later, freeing herself from the inspector's embrace.

'I don't think so,' said Montalbano, whose nostrils were filled with the scent of her skin.

'Oh my God!' Livia exclaimed, running to turn off the gas.

Montalbano had scarcely twenty minutes to shower and shave. His coffee – a fresh pot had been made in the meantime – he drank on the run, as the doorbell was already ringing. Livia didn't even ask where he was going or why. She'd opened the window and lay stretched out, arms over her head, basking in the sunlight.

＊

In the car Gallo told the inspector what he knew about the situation. The kidnapped girl – since there was no longer any doubt that she had in fact been kidnapped – was named Susanna Mistretta. A very pretty girl, she was enrolled at Palermo University and getting ready to take her first exam. She lived with her father and mother in a country villa about three miles outside of town. That was where they were heading. About a month earlier, Susanna had started going to a girlfriend's house in the early evening to study, usually driving home on her moped around eight.

The previous evening, when she didn't come home at the usual time, her father had waited about an hour before calling the girl's friend, who told him that Susanna had left as usual at eight o'clock, give or take a couple of minutes. Then he'd phoned a boy whom his daughter considered her boyfriend, and the kid seemed surprised, since he'd seen Susanna in the afternoon in Vigàta, before she went to study with her friend, and the girl had told him she wouldn't be coming with him to the movies that evening because she had to go home to study.

At this point the father started to get worried. He'd tried reaching his daughter several times on her mobile, but every time the phone was turned off. At a certain point the home phone rang, and the father rushed to pick it up, thinking it was Susanna. But it was the brother.

'Susanna has a brother?'

'No, she's an only child.'

'So, whose brother was it?' Montalbano asked in exasperation. Between Gallo's speeding and the pothole-riven road they were travelling on, not only was his head numb, but the wound in his shoulder was throbbing.

The brother in question was the brother of the father of the kidnapped girl.

'Don't any of these people have names?' asked the inspector, losing patience, hoping that knowing their names might help him follow the story a little better.

'Of course they do, why wouldn't they? It's just that nobody told me what they are,' said Gallo. He went on: 'Anyway, the kidnapped girl's father's brother, who's a doctor—'

'Just call him the doctor uncle,' Montalbano suggested.

The doctor uncle had called to find out how his sister-in-law was doing. That is, the kidnapped girl's mother.

'Why? Is she ill?'

'Yessir, Chief. Very ill.'

'And so the father told the doctor uncle—'

'No, in this case you should say his brother.'

Anyway, the father told his brother that Susanna had disappeared and asked him to come to the house to lend a hand with his sick wife, to free him up so he could look for his daughter. But the doctor had to take care of some obligations first, and it was already past eleven when he arrived.

The father then got in his car and very slowly retraced the route that Susanna normally took to go home. At that hour in winter there wasn't a soul to be seen anywhere, and very few cars. He went back and forth along the same route a second time, feeling more and more bereft of hope. At a certain point a motorbike pulled up beside him. It was Susanna's boyfriend, who had phoned the villa and was told by the doctor uncle that there still was no news. The kid told the father that he planned to scour every street in Vigàta, to see if he could at least find Susanna's motorbike, which he knew well. The father retraced Susanna's route from her friend's house to his own home four more times, occasionally stopping to examine even the spots on the pavement. But he seemed not to notice anything unusual. By the time he gave up and went home, it was almost three o'clock in the morning. At this point he suggested that his doctor brother phone all the hospitals in Vigàta and Montelusa, telling them who he was. But they all answered in the negative, which on the one hand set their minds at rest, but on the other alarmed them even further. Thus they wasted another hour.

At this point in the story – they'd been driving in the open countryside for a while and were now on an unmade road – Gallo pointed to a house about fifty yards ahead.

'That's the villa.'

Montalbano didn't have time to look at it, however, because Gallo suddenly turned right, onto another unmade road, this one in pretty bad shape.

'Where are we going?'

'To where they found the motorbike.'

It was Susanna's boyfriend who had found it. After searching in vain up and down the streets of Vigàta, he'd taken a much longer route back to the villa. And there, about two hundred yards from Susanna's house, he'd spotted the abandoned moped and run to tell the father.

Gallo pulled up, stopping behind the other squad car. When Montalbano got out, Mimì Augello came up to him.

'I don't like the smell of this, Salvo. That's why I had to bother you. But things don't look good.'

'Where's Fazio?'

'Inside the house, with the girl's father. In case the kidnappers call.'

'Mind telling me the father's name?'

'Salvatore Mistretta.'

'What's he do?'

'Used to be a geologist. He's been halfway across the world. Here's the motorbike.'

It was leaning against a low wall outside a vegetable garden. The bike was in perfect condition, no scratches or scrapes, just a little dusty. Galluzzo was in the garden, seeing if he could find anything of interest. Imbrò and Battiato were doing the same along the road.

'Susanna's boyfriend ... what's his name?'

'Francesco Lipari.'

'Where is he?'

'I sent him home. He was exhausted and worried to death.'

'I was thinking. You don't think maybe it was Lipari himself who moved the motorbike? Maybe he found it on the ground, in the middle of the road—'

'No, Salvo. He swore up and down that he found it exactly the way you see it there.'

'Post a guard next to it. And don't let anybody touch it, or forensics will go ballistic. Have you found anything?'

'Not a thing. And to think the girl had a small knapsack with her books and things, a mobile phone, a wallet she always kept in the back pocket of her jeans, the house keys ... But nothing. It's as if she ran into somebody she knew and propped the motorbike against the wall so she could talk to him.'

Montalbano seemed not to be listening, and Mimì noticed.

'What is it, Salvo?'

'I don't know, but something doesn't look right to me,' Montalbano muttered.

And he started taking a few steps backward, as one does to get a better look at something, to take it all in from the right angle. Augello also stepped back, but only mechanically, because the inspector had done so.

'It's backwards,' Montalbano concluded a moment later.

'What is?'

'The motorbike. Look at it, Mimì. The way we see it right now, at a standstill, we should think it was going to Vigàta.'

Mimì looked, then shook his head.

'That's true. But on that side of the road, it would be going the wrong way. If it was going in the direction of Vigàta, it should be on the other side, leaning against the wall opposite.'

'As if a moped cared if it was going the wrong way! Hell, you find those things on the landing outside your apartment! They'll drive right through your legs if they can! Forget about it. But if the girl was coming from Vigàta, the front wheel of the motorbike should be pointed in the opposite direction. So my question is: why is the bike positioned the way it is?'

'Jesus, Salvo, there could be a lot of reasons for that. Maybe she turned the bike around to prop it up a little better against the wall ... Or maybe she herself turned around after she saw someone she recognized—'

'Anything is possible,' Montalbano cut him off. 'I'm going over to the house. Come and join me after you've finished searching here. And don't forget to post a guard.'

✻

The villa was a two-storey building and must have once been rather beautiful. Now, however, it showed signs of neglect. And when one loses interest in a house, it can tell, and it seems to plunge into a kind of premature old age. The sturdy wrought-iron gate was ajar.

The inspector entered a large living room furnished with dark, massive nineteenth-century antiques, but at first glance it looked like a museum, as it was full of small Pre-Columbian statues and African masks. Travel souvenirs of the geologist Salvatore Mistretta. In one corner of the room there were two armchairs, a small table with a telephone on top, and a television. Fazio and a man who must have been Mistretta were sitting in the armchairs, eyes glued to the television screen. When Montalbano entered, the man gave Fazio a questioning look.

'This is Inspector Montalbano. And this is Signor Mistretta.'

The man came forward with his hand extended. Montalbano shook it without speaking. The geologist was a thin man of about sixty, with a face as baked as one of those South American statuettes, stooped shoulders, a mop of white hair, and a pair of blue eyes that wandered around the room like a drug addict's. Apparently the tension was eating away at him.

'No news?' asked Montalbano.

The geologist threw his hands up disconsolately.

'I'd like to have a word with you,' the inspector went on. 'Could we go outside?'

For no apparent reason he felt like he couldn't breathe. It was stuffy in the living room, and not a ray of light filtered in, despite two big French doors. Mistretta hesitated, then turned to Fazio.

'If somebody rings the bell upstairs, could you please let me know?'

'Of course,' said Fazio.

They went out. The garden surrounding the villa was in a state of utter abandon, now little more than a field of wild, yellowing plants.

'This way,' said the geologist.

He led the inspector to a hemicycle of wooden benches at the centre of a kind of orderly, well-tended oasis of green.

'This is where Susanna comes to stu—'

Unable to continue, he collapsed onto a bench. The inspector sat down beside him and pulled out a packet of cigarettes.

'Do you smoke?'

What had Dr Strazzera advised him to do? 'Try to stop smoking, if possible.'

At the moment, it was not possible.

'I'd stopped, but in these circumstances...' said Mistretta.

You see, dear distinguished Dr Strazzera? Sometimes one simply cannot do without it.

The inspector held out a cigarette for him and then lit it. They smoked awhile in silence, then Montalbano asked:

'Is your wife ill?'

'She's dying.'

'Does she know what's happened?'

'No. She's on tranquillizers and sedatives. My brother Carlo, who's a doctor, spent last night with her. He just left, in fact. But...'

'But?'

'But my wife, even in this induced state of sleep, keeps calling for Susanna, as if she mysteriously understands that something...'

The inspector felt himself sweating. How was he ever going to talk to the man about his daughter's kidnapping when his wife was dying? The only way, perhaps, was to adopt an official, bureaucratic tone, the kind of tone that precludes, by its very nature, any form of humanity.

'Mr Mistretta, I have to inform those in charge about the kidnapping. The judge, the commissioner, my colleagues in Montelusa ... And you can rest assured that the news will also reach the ears of some newsman who will race here with the inevitable camera crew ... The reason I'm stalling is that I want to be absolutely certain.'

'Certain of what?'

'That it's really a kidnapping we're dealing with.'

THREE

The geologist gave him a puzzled look.

'What else could it be?'

'Let me first say that I have no choice but to make conjectures, however unpleasant.'

'I understand.'

'One question. Does your wife need a lot of care?'

'Non-stop, day and night.'

'Who looks after her?'

'Susanna and I take turns.'

'How long has she been in this condition?'

'Things got worse about six months ago.'

'Is it possible that after being frayed for so long, Susanna's nerves finally gave out?'

'What are you trying to say?'

'Isn't it possible that, seeing her mother always in that state, your daughter got so worn out from all the sleepless nights and study that she ran away of her own free will from what had become an unbearable situation?'

The reply didn't come immediately.

'That's out of the question. Susanna is strong and generous. She would never do that to me. Never. And anyway, where would she hide?'

'Did she have any money on her?'

'I dunno, maybe thirty euros, at the most.'

'Doesn't she have any relatives or friends she's particularly fond of?'

'There's only my brother, whom she would visit at his house, but not very often. And she would meet with that boy who helped me in my search. They'd often go to the movies together or out for pizza. But there's nobody else she was close to.'

'What about the girl she was studying with?'

'She's just a study companion, I think.'

Now they came to the difficult part, and the inspector had to be careful not to further offend this wounded man with his questions. He took a deep breath. The morning air was, in spite of everything, sweet and fragrant.

'Listen, your daughter's boyfriend . . . what's his name?'

'Francesco. Francesco Lipari.'

'Did Susanna get along well with Francesco?'

'As far as I could tell, yes, basically.'

'What do you mean by "basically"?'

'I mean that sometimes I would hear her arguing with him over the telephone . . . But just silly stuff, the kind of things young lovers quarrel about.'

'You don't think that Susanna perhaps met someone who secretly lured her, persuading her to—'

'To go with him, you mean? Inspector, Susanna has always been a sincere, forthright girl. If she'd started up a relationship with someone else, she would certainly have told Francesco and broken up with him.'

'So you're sure we're dealing with a kidnapping.'

'Unfortunately, yes.'

Fazio suddenly appeared in the doorway of the villa.

'What is it?' asked the geologist.

'I heard the bell ring upstairs.'

Mistretta rushed inside. Montalbano followed slowly behind him, lost in thought. He went back into the living room and sat down in the empty armchair in front of the telephone.

'Poor guy,' said Fazio. 'I feel sorry for this Mistretta, I really do.'

'Doesn't it seem strange to you that the kidnappers haven't called yet? It's almost ten o'clock.'

'I don't know much about kidnappings,' said Fazio.

'Me neither. And Mimì doesn't either.'

Speak of the devil. At that very moment Mimì Augello walked in.

'We didn't find anything. What do we do now?'

'Inform everyone we're supposed to inform about the kidnapping. Give me Susanna's boyfriend's address, and the address of the girl she was studying with.'

'What are you going to do?' asked Mimì as he was writing these things down on a piece of paper.

'As soon as he returns, I'm going to say goodbye to Mr Mistretta and go to the office.'

'But aren't you convalescing?' asked Mimì. 'I only had you come here to give advice, not to—'

'And do you feel confident leaving the station in Catarella's hands?'

There was no answer, only a troubled silence.

'If the kidnappers get in touch soon, as I'm hoping they'll do, let me know at once,' the inspector said in a decisive tone.

'Why are you hoping the kidnappers get in touch soon?' asked Fazio.

Before answering, the inspector read the piece of paper Augello had handed to him, then put it in his pocket.

'Because that way we'll know that they kidnapped her for money. Let's be frank. A girl like Susanna gets kidnapped for one of two reasons: for money or for rape. Gallo told me she's a very attractive girl. In the latter case, the chances she'd be killed after being raped are very high.'

A chill. In the silence they could hear the geologist's shuffling footsteps as he approached. He looked at Augello.

'Did you find any...?'

Mimì shook his head.

Mistretta staggered as though dizzy, but Mimì quickly steadied him.

'But why did they do it? Why?!' he said, burying his face in his hands.

'Why?' said Augello, hoping to console him with words. 'You'll see, they'll probably demand a ransom, the judge very probably will allow you to pay, and—'

'What will I pay with? How can I pay?' the man cried in desperation. 'Doesn't everyone know that we get by on my pension? And that the only thing we own is this house?'

Montalbano was standing near Fazio. He heard him whisper under his breath:

'*Matre santa!* So . . .'

*

He had Gallo drop him off at Susanna's study-companion's place. The girl went by the name of Tina Lofaro and lived on the town's main street in a three-storey building that, like most of the buildings in the centre of town, was rather old. As the inspector was about to ring the intercom, the front door opened and out came a woman of about fifty, trailing an empty shopping trolley behind her.

'Please leave the door open,' Montalbano said to her.

The woman hesitated a moment, reaching behind her with one arm to hold the door open, torn between courtesy and caution. But after looking him up and down, she made up her mind and walked away. The inspector went in and closed the door behind him. There was no lift. On the postboxes, the Lofaro family's residence corresponded to apartment number six, and since there were two flats per floor, that meant that he would have to climb up three flights of stairs. He had purposely avoided letting them know he was coming. He knew from experience that an unannounced visit from a man of the law always provokes at least a little unease, even in the most honest of people, who immediately wonder: What have I done wrong? Because all honest people believe that at one time or another they have done something wrong, perhaps without even realizing, whereas dishonest people are always convinced they've acted honestly. Therefore all of them, honest and dishonest, feel uneasy. And this helps one find the chinks in everyone's armour.

The inspector thus hoped, when ringing the doorbell, that Tina herself would answer. Caught by surprise, the girl would certainly reveal whether or not Susanna had told her some little secret that might help the investigation.

The door opened, and there appeared a short, plain girl of about twenty, dark as a crow, chubby and wearing thick spectacles. Tina, surely. The element of surprise worked. But in reverse.

'I'm Inspector Mon—'

'—talbano!' said Tina, a big smile cleaving her face from ear to ear. 'Wow! How cool! I never thought I'd meet you! Cool! I'm so excited I'm starting to sweat! I'm so happy!'

Montalbano couldn't move. He looked like he'd turned into a puppet without strings. To his bewilderment, he noticed a strange phenomenon. The girl before him had started to evaporate. A cloud of steam was enveloping her. Tina was melting like a pat of butter in the summer sun. The girl then extended a sweaty hand, grabbed the inspector by the wrist, pulled him inside, and closed the door. Then she stood there in front of him, speechless and ecstatic, face red as a ripe watermelon, hands joined in prayer, eyes glistening. For a brief moment, Montalbano felt exactly like the Blessed Virgin of Pompeii.

'I would like—' he ventured.

'Of course! I'm so sorry! Come!' said Tina, rousing herself from her ecstasy and leading him into the inevitable sitting room. 'Wow, the moment I saw you there before me in the flesh, I nearly fainted! How are you? Have you recovered? This is amazing! I always see you when you appear on TV, you know. And I read a lot of detective novels, I just love them, but you, Inspector, you're a lot better than Maigret, or Poirot, or ... You want a coffee?'

'Who?' asked Montalbano, dazed.

Since the girl had spoken almost without interruption, the inspector had heard only something like 'Uwanakafi', thinking this might be the protagonist detective of some African writer with whom he was unfamiliar.

'So, will you have some coffee?'

Maybe it was just the thing.

'Yes, if it isn't a bother . . .'

'Not at all! Mama went out shopping about five minutes ago and I'm all alone because the housekeeper's not coming today, but I can have it ready for you in a jiffy!'

She disappeared. So they were alone in the house? The inspector got worried. This girl was capable of anything. From the kitchen he heard a clinking of demitasses and saucers and a sort of low murmur. Who was she talking to, since she'd said there was nobody else in the house? Herself? He got up and went out of the living room. The kitchen was the second door on the left. He approached slowly, on tiptoe. Tina was talking in a low voice on her mobile.

'. . . he's here, I tell you! I'm not kidding! All of a sudden, there he was, right in front of me! If you can get here within ten minutes, he'll still be here, I promise. Oh and, listen, Sandra, be sure to tell Manuela, I'm sure she'll want to come, too. And bring a camera, so we can all take our pictures with him.'

Montalbano retraced his steps. This was all he needed! Three twenty-year-old girls attacking him like some rock star! He decided he would shake free of Tina in less than ten minutes. He drank the coffee boiling hot, scalding his lips, and began his questioning. But the element of surprise hadn't worked, and the inspector gained little or nothing from the conversation.

'No, I wouldn't say friends as in *real* friends. We met at the university, and when we found out we both lived in Vigàta, we decided to study together for our first exam, and now for the last month or so she's been coming to my house every evening from five to eight...'

'Yes, I think she's very fond of Francesco...'

'No, she never mentioned any other boys to me...'

'No, she never said anything to me about any other guys coming on to her...'

'Susanna is generous and sincere, but I wouldn't say she's very expansive. She tends to hold everything inside...'

'No, yesterday she went away like every other day. And we agreed to meet again today at five...'

'Lately she's been the same as usual. Her mother's health has been a constant worry. Normally around seven we would take a break from our study, and Susanna would phone home and find out how her mother was doing ... Yes, she did the same yesterday...'

'Inspector, I really don't think she was kidnapped. I feel pretty good about that. Oh God, it's so cool being interrogated by you! You want to know what I think? Jesus, this is so fabulous! The inspector wants to know what I think! OK, I think Susanna went away of her own accord and will come back in a few days. She probably needed a little rest and couldn't handle watching her mother die that way, day after day, night after night . . .'

'What, are you leaving already? Don't you want to interrogate me some more? Couldn't you wait another five minutes, so we can take our picture together? Aren't you going to summon me down to the station? You're not?'

She suddenly stood up, seeing the inspector do the same. Then she made a move that Montalbano mistakenly interpreted as the start of a belly dance.

'OK, OK, I'll summon you down to the station,' he said, racing toward the door.

*

Seeing the inspector appear unexpectedly before him, Catarella nearly fainted.

'Jesus, what a pleasant s'prise! Jesus, iss so nice t'see you all over again, Chief!'

No sooner had Montalbano entered his office than the door slammed violently against the wall. Since he was no longer used to this, the inspector took fright.

'What's going on?'

A panting Catarella stood in the doorway.

'Nuttin', Chief. My hand slipped.'

'What do you want?'

'Ahh, Chief! I'm so ixcited t'see you that I forgot ta tell ya that the c'mishner called looking for you. Iss rilly rilly urgint!'

'OK, ring him up and put him through to me.'

'Hello, Montalbano? First of all, how are you?'

'Pretty well, thanks.'

'I took the liberty of calling you at home, but your
... the lady told me ... and so I ...'

'What can I do for you, sir?'

'I heard about the kidnapping. A nasty business, it
seems.'

'Very nasty.'

Hyperbole always worked with the commissioner.
But what was he driving at with this phone call?

'Well, here's the thing ... I'd like you to come
back to active duty – just for the moment, of course,
and assuming, also, that you're up to ... Sooner or later,
Inspector Augello will have to go out in the field to coordinate the searches, and I haven't got anyone to replace
him in Vigàta ... Do you understand?'

'Of course.'

'Excellent. So I'm officially informing you that the
kidnapping investigation will be handled by Inspector
Minutolo, who, being a Calabrian ...' – What? Minutolo
was from Alì, in Messina province – '...should know a
lot about kidnappings.'

Thus – strictly applying Commissioner Bonetti-
Alderighi's logic – one needed only to be Chinese to
know a lot about Chinese chequers.

'Now you,' the commissioner went on, 'don't go
treading on other people's turf the way you always do.

I mean it. I want you only to lend support, or, at most, to carry on some minor side investigations that won't wear you out but will converge with Minutolo's central investigation.'

'Could you give me a practical example?'

'Of what?'

'Of how I might converge with Inspector Minutolo.'

He enjoyed acting like a complete idiot with the commissioner. The only problem was that the commissioner really believed he was a complete idiot. Bonetti-Alderighi sighed so loudly that Montalbano heard him. Perhaps it was better not to take the game too far.

'Sorry, sorry, I think I understand. If Inspector Minutolo's conducting the main investigation, that would make him the Po, whereas I would be the Dora, the Riparia, or the Baltea, it makes no difference. Right?'

'Right,' the commissioner said wearily. Then he hung up.

The only positive thing to come out of all this was that the investigation had been turned over to Filippo Minutolo, known as Fifì, an intelligent man with whom one could reason.

Montalbano phoned Livia to tell her he'd been called back to duty, if only in the role of Dora Riparia (or was it Baltea?). But she didn't answer. No doubt she'd taken the car and gone to the museum or for a stroll in the Valley of the Temples, as she always did when she came to Vigàta. He rang her mobile, but it was turned off.

More precisely, the recording said the person he was
calling could not be reached. And it advised him to try
again later. But how can one reach somebody who can't
be reached? Just by trying again later? As a rule, the
telephone people tended toward absurdity. They said,
for example: *The number you have reached does not exist* ...
How could they possibly say such a thing? Every number
that one can think of exists. If a number, even one, in
the infinite sequence of numbers were missing, the entire
universe would be plunged into chaos. Didn't the telephone companies realize this?

Whatever the case, it was now time to eat, but there
was no point in going back to Marinella. He wouldn't
find anything made by Adelina in the fridge or the oven.
Informed that Livia was staying at the house, the housekeeper would not show up again until Livia was certifiably
gone. The two women disliked each other too much.

He was getting up to go and eat at the Trattoria Da
Enzo when Catarella told him Inspector Minutolo was on
the line.

'Any news, Fifi?'

'Nothing, Salvo. I'm calling about Fazio.'

'What's up?'

'Could I borrow him? Because the commissioner hasn't
given me a single man for this investigation, only tech-
nicians, who just bugged the Lofaros' phone and then left.
He said I should be able to go it alone.'

'Because you're Calabrian and therefore an expert in kidnappings. That's what he told me.'

Minutolo muttered something that didn't sound like unmitigated praise for his superior.

'So, can I borrow him at least until this evening?'

'If he doesn't collapse first. Listen, don't you think it's strange the kidnappers haven't made contact yet?'

'No, not at all. I once had a case, in Sardinia, where they didn't deign to send a message until a week after the kidnapping, and then another time—'

'You see? You are an expert, after all, just as the commissioner said.'

'Go and fuck yourselves, both of you!'

*

Montalbano disgracefully took advantage of the free time and the fact that Livia was incommunicado.

'Welcome back, Inspector! You picked the right day to come!' said Enzo.

As an exceptional treat, Enzo had made couscous with eight different kinds of fish, but only for his favourite customers. These, of course, included the inspector, who, the moment he saw the dish in front of him and inhaled its aroma, was overcome with emotion. Enzo noticed but, luckily, misunderstood.

'Your eyes are shining, Inspector! Got a touch of fever, by any chance?'

'Yes,' he lied without hesitation.

He scarfed down two helpings. Afterwards, he shame-
lessly declared that a few little mullets might be a nice
idea. A stroll out to the lighthouse at the end of the jetty
thus became a digestive necessity.

Back at the station, he phoned Livia again. The
recording repeated that the person could not be reached.
Oh well.

Galluzzo came in to report on a case involving a
supermarket robbery.

'Excuse me, but isn't Inspector Augello here?'

'Yes, Chief, he's over there.'

'Well then, go over there and tell him about it. Before
he gets called into the field, as the commissioner put it.'

*

There was no getting around it, Susanna's disappearance
was beginning to worry him in earnest. His real fear was
that the girl had been kidnapped by a sex maniac. Maybe
it was best to advise Minutolo to organize a search team
immediately, without waiting for a phone call that might
never come.

He took the scrap of paper Mimì had given him out
of his pocket and dialled the number of Susanna's
boyfriend.

'Hello, is this the Lipari home? This is Inspector Montalbano. I'd like to speak to Francesco.'

'Oh, it's you? This is Francesco, Inspector.'

There was a note of disappointment in his voice. Apparently he was hoping it would be Susanna calling.

'Listen, could you come and see me?'

'When?'

'Right now, if possible.'

'Is there any news?'

This time anxiety had replaced disappointment.

'No, but I'd like to talk with you a little.'

'I'll be right over.'

FOUR

Francesco arrived barely ten minutes later.

'It's pretty quick with a motorbike,' he said.

A good-looking kid, tall, well dressed, with a clear, open gaze. But one could see that he was being eaten alive by worry. He sat down on the edge of a chair, nerves taut.

'Have you already been questioned by my colleague Minutolo?'

'I haven't been questioned by anybody. I phoned Susanna's father late this morning to find out if ... but unfortunately ...'

He stopped and looked the inspector straight in the eye.

'And this silence makes me imagine the worst.'

'Such as?'

'That maybe she's been kidnapped by someone who wants to abuse her. And that she's either still in his hands or else he's already ...'

'What makes you think this?'

'Inspector, everyone knows that Susanna's father doesn't have a cent. He used to be rich, but he had to sell everything.'

'Why? Did his business go bad?'

'I don't know why. But he wasn't a businessman. He earned a good salary and had put a lot of money aside. And I think Susanna's mother also inherited a ... well, I don't know, frankly.'

'Go on.'

'As I was saying, do you really think the kidnappers would be unaware of the victim's economic situation? Would they make that kind of mistake? Come on! They know more about us than the tax collectors!'

The argument made sense.

'And there's another thing,' the kid went on. 'I've waited for Susanna outside Tina's place at least four or five different times. After she came out, we would head back to her house on our motorbikes. Now and then we would stop, then we'd continue on our way. When we arrived at the gate we would say goodbye and I'd go home. We always took the same route. The most direct one, which Susanna always took. Whereas last night she took a different road, more out of the way. It's full of holes, almost impassable. You need a four-by-four to get through there. There's hardly any light, and it's much longer than our usual route. I have no idea why she would go that way. But it's an ideal place for a kidnapping. Maybe it was a chance encounter that went bad.'

The boy had a good head on his shoulders.

'How old are you, young man?'

'Twenty-three. You can call me Francesco, if you want. You're old enough to be my father.'

With a pang to the heart, Montalbano realized that, at this stage of his life, he would never be the father of a kid that age.

'Are you a student?'

'Yes, in law. I graduate next year.'

'What do you want to do in life?'

He asked only to relieve the tension.

'The same thing you do.'

Montalbano thought he hadn't heard right.

'You want to join the police force?'

'Yes.'

'Why?'

'Because I like it.'

'I wish you the best of luck. Listen, to get back to your rapist hypothesis ... which, mind you, is only a hypothesis.'

'Which I'm sure you'd already thought of.'

'Of course. Did Susanna ever mention people making lewd propositions, obscene phone calls, things like that?'

'Susanna's very reserved. She certainly got a lot of compliments, wherever she went. She's a beautiful girl. Sometimes she would repeat them to me, and we would laugh about it. If there was any cause for worry, I'm sure she would have mentioned it to me.'

'Her friend Tina is convinced Susanna ran away of her own volition.'

Francesco gave him an astonished look, mouth open.

'Why would she do that?'

'A sudden breakdown. The pain and tension caused by her mother's illness, the physical strain of caring for her, the stress of studying for exams. Is Susanna a fragile girl?'

'So that's what Tina thinks? She obviously doesn't know Susanna! Susanna's nerves are bound to give out, that much is certain, but it's equally certain the break-down won't come until after her mother dies! Until that moment, she will stay at her bedside. Because once she gets something in her head, and she's convinced she's right, she becomes so determined that ... She's anything but fragile! No, believe me, that's an absurd hypothesis.'

'Speaking of which, what is Susanna's mother ill with?'

'To be perfectly honest, Inspector, I don't know what's wrong with her. A couple of weeks ago, Susanna's uncle, Carlo, the doctor, had some sort of consultation with two doctors — one who'd come down from Rome, the other from Milan — and in the end they all threw their hands up. Susanna explained to me that her mother is dying of an incurable disease: the refusal to live. A kind of fatal depression. When I asked the reason for this depression — since I believe there always has to be a reason — she answered evasively.'

Montalbano steered the conversation back to the girl.

'How did you meet Susanna?'

'Purely by chance, in a bar. She was with a girl I used to go out with.'

'When was this?'

'About six months ago.'

'And you hit it off straightaway?'

Francesco gave a broad smile.

'It was love at first sight.'

'Do you do it?'

'Do what?'

'Make love.'

'Yes.'

'Where?'

'At my place.'

'Do you live alone?'

'I live with my father. But he's away a lot, often travels abroad. He's a wholesaler in timber. He's in Russia at the moment.'

'What about your mother?'

'They're divorced. My mother's remarried and lives in Siracusa.'

Francesco opened and then closed his mouth, as if he wanted to add something.

'Go on,' Montalbano prodded him.

'But we don't ...'

'Say it.'

The kid hesitated. It was clear he felt embarrassed talking about something so private.

'You'll see,' the inspector continued, 'when you become a policeman yourself, you too will have to ask indiscreet questions.'

'I know. I merely wanted to say that we don't do it very often.'

'She doesn't want to?'

'No, not exactly. I'm always the one who asks her to come to my place. But every time I've felt as though, I don't know, she seemed distant, or absent. It was like she went along with it just to please me. I realized that she's very affected by her mother's illness. And I felt ashamed to ask her . . . Just yesterday afternoon—'

He broke off, then made a strange face, as though perplexed.

'How strange . . .' Francesco muttered.

The inspector pricked his ears.

'Just yesterday afternoon?' he pressed.

'She was the one who suggested we go to my place. And I said yes. We didn't have much time, since she'd been at the bank and then had to go to Tina's to study.'

The kid still looked bewildered.

'Maybe she wanted to reward you for your patience,' said Montalbano.

'Yeah, you're probably right. Because this time, for the first time, Susanna was present. Entirely present. With me. Do you understand?'

'Yes. Sorry, but you said that before meeting you, she'd been to the bank. Do you know why she went?'

'She had to withdraw some money.'

'And did she?'

'Of course.'

'Do you know how much?'

'No.'

So why had Susanna's father said that she had only thirty euros, at the most, in her pocket? Maybe he didn't know she'd been to the bank? The inspector stood up, and the young man did the same.

'OK, Francesco, you can go. It's been a real pleasure to meet you. I'll give you a ring if I need you.'

He held out his hand, and Francesco shook it.

'Could I ask you one thing?' the boy asked.

'Of course.'

'Why, in your opinion, was Susanna's motorbike parked that way?'

This Francesco Lipari would make a good policeman, no doubt about it.

*

He phoned Marinella. Livia had just come in and was happy.

'You know what?' she said. 'I've just discovered a fabulous place. It's called Kolymbetra. Just think, it used to be a great big pool, originally carved out by Carthaginian prisoners.'

'Where is it?'

'It's right there, near the temples. Now it's a kind of vast garden of Eden, just recently opened to the public.'

'Did you have lunch?'

'No, just a panino at Kolymbetra. How about you?'

'Nah, all I had was a panino, too.'

The lie had come out spontaneously, without warning. Why hadn't he told her he'd gorged himself on couscous and mullets, violating the sort of diet that Livia was forcing him to follow? For what reason? Perhaps a combination of shame, cowardice, and a desire to avoid a quarrel.

'Poor thing! Will you be back late?'

'I really don't think so.'

'Then I'll cook something.'

Here was the instant punishment for his lie. He would expiate his sin by eating a dinner prepared by Livia. Not that she was a terrible cook, but her dishes tended toward the flavourless, the spiceless, the lightest of light, the I-can-but-I-can't-really-taste-it. Instead of actually cooking, Livia hinted at cooking.

He decided to drop in at the villa to see how things were going. He drove off, and then, as he drew near, he noticed that traffic was getting heavy. In fact there were a good ten cars parked along the road that ran along one side of the villa, and in front of the closed gate six or seven people jostled about, camcorders on their shoulders, trying to get a good shot of the lane and the garden.

Montalbano closed the windows of his car and drove forward, wildly honking his horn, until he nearly crashed into the gate.

'Inspector! Inspector Montalbano!'

Muffled voices called out to him; some idiot photographer blinded him with a burst of flashes. Luckily the Montelusa policeman standing guard recognized him and opened the gate. The inspector drove his car inside, pulled up, and got out.

He found Fazio sitting in the usual armchair in the living room, pale-faced, hollow-eyed, and looking generally very tired. His eyes were closed, head thrown back and resting against the back of the chair. A variety of gadgets were now attached to the phone, including a tape recorder and headset. A uniformed policeman, not from the Vigàta force, was standing near a French door, thumbing through a magazine. The moment the inspector entered, the telephone rang. Fazio leapt up, and in the twinkling of an eye had donned the headset, started the tape recorder, and picked up the receiver.

'Hello?'

He listened for a moment.

'No, Mr Mistretta is not at home ... No, please don't insist.'

He hung up and saw the inspector. He removed the headset and stood up.

'Oh, Chief! The phone's been ringing non-stop for

the last three hours! My head is numb! I don't know how it happened, but everybody, all over Italy, knows about this disappearance, and they're all calling to interview the poor father!'

'Where's Inspector Minutolo?'

'He's back in Montelusa, packing an overnight bag. He's gonna sleep here tonight. He just left.'

'What about Mistretta?'

'He just went upstairs to be with his wife. He woke up about an hour ago.'

'He was able to sleep?'

'Not for long, but he was given something. At lunch-time his brother the doctor turned up with a nurse who's going to spend the night with the sick wife. Then the doctor gave his brother a sedative injection. You know, Chief, there was some kind of argument between the two brothers.'

'He didn't want the injection?'

'Well, that too, but first Mr Mistretta got upset when he saw the nurse. He told his brother he didn't have the money to pay her, to which his brother replied that he would pay for it himself. Then Mistretta started crying, saying he was reduced to living on other people's charity . . . Poor man, I really do feel sorry for him.'

'Listen Fazio, sorry or not, tonight you're going to clock off, go home, and get some rest. OK?'

'OK, OK. Here's Mr Mistretta.'

The sleep hadn't done him any good. He was swaying as he walked, weak-kneed and hands trembling. Seeing Montalbano, he became alarmed.

'Oh my God! What's happened?'

'Nothing, I assure you. Please don't get excited. But since I'm here, I'd like to ask you a question. Do you feel up to answering?'

'I'll try.'

'Thank you. Do you remember that this morning you told me Susanna could only have had thirty euros, at most, on her? Was that the amount your daughter usually went around with?'

'Yes, I can confirm that. That's more or less how much she usually had on her.'

'Did you know that she went to the bank yesterday afternoon?'

Mistretta looked stunned.

'In the afternoon? No, I didn't know. Who told you that?'

'Francesco, Susanna's boyfriend.'

Mistretta looked sincerely bewildered. He sat down in the first chair that came within reach and ran a hand over his brow. He was trying very hard to understand.

'Unless . . .' he muttered.

'Unless what?'

'Well, yesterday morning I told Susanna to go to the bank to see if some back payments had been credited to my pension. The account is in both of our names, mine and hers. If the money was there, she was supposed to withdraw three thousand euros and pay off some debts that, frankly, I didn't want to think about any more. They weighed on my mind.'

'What kind of debts, if you don't mind my asking?'

'I dunno, the chemist, some shopkeepers ... Not that they ever put any pressure on us, but it was I who ... But when Susanna came home around noon, I didn't ask her whether she'd been to the bank, so maybe ...'

'Maybe she'd forgotten to do it and didn't remember until the afternoon,' the inspector finished his sentence for him.

'I'm sure that's what happened,' said Mistretta.

'But that means that Susanna had three thousand or more euros on her person. Which isn't a whole lot, of course, but to an imbecile ...'

'But she would have paid the bills with it!'

'No, she didn't.'

'How can you be so sure?'

'Because when she came out of the bank she ... stopped to talk with Francesco.'

'Oh.'

Then he clapped his hands together. 'But ... we can call and check ...'

Mistretta got up wearily, went over to the phone, dialled a number, then spoke in a voice so soft that all they could hear were the words:

'Hello? Bevilacqua Chemist's?'

He hung up almost at once.

'You were right, Inspector, she didn't stop at the chemist's to pay off our outstanding bill ... And if she didn't go to the chemist's, she probably didn't go anywhere else.'

Then all at once, he cried out:

'*O Madonna mia!*'

It seemed impossible, but his face, which was pale as could be, somehow managed to turn even paler. Montalbano worried that the man might be having a stroke.

'What's wrong?'

'Now they won't believe me!' Mistretta moaned.

'Who won't believe you?'

'The kidnappers! Because I told a journalist—'

'What journalist? Did you talk to journalists?'

'Yes, but only to one. Inspector Minutolo said I could.'

'But why, for the love of God?'

Mistretta looked at him, befuddled.

'Wasn't I supposed to? I wanted to send a message to the kidnappers.... To say that they were making a terrible mistake, that I haven't got any money to pay the ransom ... And now they're going to find three thousand ... Can you imagine, a young girl going around with all that money in her pocket? They'll never believe me! Poor ... girl ... My poor daughter!'

Sobbing prevented him from going on, but as far as the inspector was concerned, he'd said more than enough.

'Good day,' Montalbano said.

And he stalked out of the living room, in the grips of an uncontrollable rage. What the hell was Minutolo thinking when he authorized him to make that declaration? He could already imagine how the newspapers, television, and everybody else would embroider the story! The kidnappers would likely now turn nasty, and the person who would suffer the most would be poor Susanna. Assuming there was, in fact, a ransom to be paid. From the garden, he called to the policeman who was reading near the French door.

'Go and tell your colleague to hold the gate open for me.'

He got in his car, turned on the ignition, waited a few seconds, then took off like Schumacher in a Formula I race. The journalists and cameramen scattered in every direction, cursing.

'Is he crazy? Is he trying to kill us?'

Instead of continuing down the same road he'd come in on, he turned left onto the unmade road where the motorbike had been found. And in fact the road was impassable for a normal vehicle. He had to drive as slowly as possible and continually perform complicated manoeuvres to keep the wheels from plunging into huge trenches and hollows of the sort one might find between dunes in the desert. But the worst was yet to come. Less than half a mile before the outskirts of town, the road was cut off by an enormous excavation pit. Apparently one of those 'roadworks ahead' that in Italy have the peculiarity of always lying ahead even when the whole world has passed them by. To get past it, Susanna must have got off her motorbike and walked it around the pit, or else had to make an even wider detour, since those who'd passed through before her had, by dint of going repeatedly back and forth, created a kind of bypass trail through the open countryside. But what did it mean? Why had Susanna taken this route? He had an idea. With a series of manoeuvres so exacting and numerous that his injured shoulder began to ache again, he turned the car around and headed back. The unmade road was starting to seem endless when at last he came to the main road and stopped. It was getting dark. He couldn't make up his mind. It would take at least an hour to do what he wanted to do, which meant that he would return home late, probably sparking a squabble with Livia. And he was in no mood for that. On the other hand, what he wanted to do was merely a routine check, which anyone at the station could do. He started the car up again and drove back to headquarters.

'Summon Inspector Augello to my office at once,' he ordered Catarella.

'Chief, he in't poissonally here.'

'Who is?'

'Want their names in flabbetical order?'

'Whatever order you like.'

'OK, there's Gallo, Galluzzo, Germanà, Giallombardo, Grasso, Imbrò . . .'

He chose Gallo.

'What can I do for you, Chief?'

'Listen, Gallo, I want you to go back to that unmade road where you took me this morning.'

'What do you want me to do?'

'There's ten or so little country houses along that road. I want you to stop at every house and ask if anyone knows Susanna Mistretta, or if they saw a girl pass by last night on a motorbike.'

'All right, Chief, I'll get on it first thing in the morning.'

'No, Gallo, perhaps I didn't make myself clear. I want you to go there immediately and then ring me at home.'

*

He arrived home feeling a little worried that Livia might give him the third degree. And indeed she started the questioning at once, after greeting him with a kiss that seemed a bit distracted to him.

'So why did you have to go in to work?'

'Because the commissioner put me back on duty.' And he added, as a precaution, 'But only temporarily.'

'Do you feel tired?'

'Not at all.'

'Did you have to drive?'

'I had the patrol car take me around.'

End of interrogation. Some third degree! This was a piece of cake with icing.

FIVE

'Did you watch the news?' he asked in turn, seeing that the danger had passed.

Livia replied that she hadn't even turned on the television. He would therefore have to wait for the ten-thirty edition of *TeleVigàta News*, since Minutolo must surely have chosen to speak to the station that was always pro-government regardless of who was in power.

Although the pasta was a tad overcooked and the sauce acidic, and although the meat looked and tasted exactly like a piece of cardboard, the dinner Livia had cooked up could not really be considered an incitement to murder. Throughout the meal, Livia spoke to him about Kolymbetra, trying to convey a little of the excitement she'd felt.

Without warning she broke off, stood up, and went out on the veranda.

It took Montalbano a few moments to realize she'd stopped speaking to him. Without getting up, and convinced that Livia had gone outside because she'd heard something, he asked her in a loud voice:

'What is it? What did you hear?'

Livia reappeared with fire in her eyes.

'Nothing, that's what I heard. What was I supposed to hear? All I heard was your silence! That was loud and clear! You never listen when I talk to you, or else you pretend to listen and then answer in an incomprehensible mumble!'

Oh, no, not a squabble! He had to dodge it at all costs. Maybe by feigning a tragic tone ... And it wouldn't be entirely staged, since there was an element of truth to it. He did, in fact, feel very tired.

'No, Livia, no ...' he said.

Resting his elbows on the table, he covered his face with his hands. Livia became alarmed and immediately changed tone.

'But be reasonable, Salvo. Whenever anybody talks to you, you just—'

'I know, I know. Please forgive me, that's just the way I am, and I don't even realize it when ...'

He spoke in a strangled voice, hands pressing hard on his eyes. Then he got up all at once and ran into the bathroom, closing the door behind him. After washing his face, he re-emerged.

Livia was standing outside the door, repentant. He'd put on a good performance. The audience was moved. They embraced with abandon, asking each other's pardon.

'I'm sorry, it's just that today was a bad—'

'I'm sorry, too, Salvo.'

They spent two hours chatting on the little veranda. Then they went back inside and the inspector turned on the television, tuning it to TeleVigàta. The kidnapping of Susanna Mistretta was naturally the lead story. As the anchorman spoke of the girl, a photograph of her appeared on the screen. At that point Montalbano realized that he'd never felt curious enough to find out what she looked like. She was a beautiful girl, blonde and blue-eyed. Little wonder that people complimented her on the street, as Francesco had mentioned. Her expression, however, was one of self-assurance and determination, which made her look slightly older than her years. Then some images of the villa appeared. The newsman hadn't the slightest doubt that Susanna had been kidnapped, despite the fact that no ransom demands had yet been made on the family. By way of conclusion, he informed viewers that the station would now show an exclusive interview with the kidnap victim's father. Mr Mistretta appeared on the screen.

The moment the man began to speak, Montalbano was flabbergasted. In front of a television camera, some people lose their train of thought, stutter, go cross-eyed, sweat, say stupid things — he himself belonged to this unhappy category — whereas others remain perfectly normal, speaking and moving the way they usually do. Then there is a third category, the chosen few who become more lucid and clear when a camera is watching. Mistretta belonged to the latter group. He said that whoever had kidnapped his daughter, Susanna, had made a mistake. Whatever sum they might ask for her liberation, the family was in no position to raise any money. The kidnappers should better inform themselves, he said. The only solution was to set Susanna free, immediately. If, however, there was something else the kidnappers wanted – though he, Mistretta, could not imagine what this might be – they should make their demands at once. He would do the impossible to satisfy them.

That was all. His voice was firm, his eyes dry. Troubled, yes, but not afraid. With this declaration, the geologist won the esteem and respect of all who had heard him.

'He's a real man, this Mistretta,' said Livia.

The anchorman reappeared, saying he would report the rest of the news after the station's commentary on what was clearly the biggest story of the day. The purse-lipped face of TeleVigàta's main editorialist, Pippo Ragonese, appeared on the screen. He started by saying that it was well known that retired geologist Salvatore Mistretta was of modest means, even though his wife, now gravely ill, had once been wealthy before losing everything in a reversal of fortune. Therefore, as the girl's poor father had said in his appeal, if the purpose of this kidnapping was money – and he, Ragonese, certainly didn't want to conjecture as to what other terrible motive might be behind it — then it had been a tragic mistake. Now who was most likely not to know that Mistretta and his family had been living in dignified poverty? Only foreigners, Third-Worlders, clearly ill-informed. For there was no denying that ever since all these illegal immigrants had been landing on these shores in what was a veritable invasion, crime rates had soared, surpassing previous high-water marks. What were local governments waiting for to strictly apply an already existing law? Personally, however, he did take comfort in one aspect of this kidnapping case. The investigation had been entrusted to the able Inspector Filippo Minutolo of Montelusa Police and not to so-called Inspector Salvo Montalbano, known more for his questionable brainstorms and his unorthodox and at times downright subversive opinions than for his ability to solve the cases assigned to him. And on that note, Ragonese wished them all a good night.

'What a bastard!' said Livia, turning off the TV.

Montalbano chose not to open his mouth. By now the things Ragonese said about him had no effect on him. The telephone rang. It was Gallo.

'I just finished, Chief. There was only one house that didn't have anyone in it, but it seemed like it hadn't been lived in for a while. And everyone gave the same answer: nobody knows Susanna and they didn't see any girl pass by on a motorbike last night. But one lady did say that the fact she didn't see anything didn't necessarily mean that a girl on a motorbike didn't pass by.'

'Why are you telling me this?'

'Because those houses have all got their gardens and kitchens at the back, not on the road side.'

He hung up. The mild disappointment made him feel tremendously weary.

'What do you say, shall we go to bed?'

'All right,' said Livia, 'but why haven't you told me anything about this kidnapping?'

Because you didn't give me the chance, he was about to say, but held himself back in time. Those words would surely have triggered a furious spat. He merely gave a vague shrug.

'Is it true you were left off the case, as that *cornuto* just said on TV?'

'Congratulations, Livia.'

'Why?'

'I can see you're becoming a true Vigatese. You called Ragonese a *cornuto*. Calling people *cornuti* is typical of aborigines.'

'I obviously caught it from you. But tell me, is it true you were—'

'Not exactly. I'm supposed to work together with Minutolo. But the investigation was his from the start. And I was on leave.'

'Tell me about the kidnapping while I tidy up.'

The inspector told her everything there was to tell. When he'd finished, Livia looked troubled.

'If they ask for a ransom, will all your other conjectures prove false?'

She, too, was thinking that they might have kidnapped Susanna in order to rape her. Montalbano wanted to tell her that a ransom demand didn't preclude rape, but he decided it was better if she went to bed without this worry on her mind.

'Of course. You want the bathroom first?'

'OK.'

Montalbano opened the French door giving onto the veranda, sat down, and lit a cigarette. The night was as placid as a baby's sleep. He managed to stop thinking about Susanna and the horror that this same night must have represented to her.

After a short spell, he heard a noise inside the house. He got up, went in, and froze. Livia was standing in the middle of the room, naked. At her feet was a small puddle of water. Apparently something had occurred to her halfway through the shower and she'd stepped out. She looked beautiful, but Montalbano didn't dare make a move. Livia's eyes, reduced to mere slits, heralded an impending storm.

'You ... you ...' said Livia, her arm extended, pointing an accusing finger.

'Me what?'

'When did you learn about the kidnapping?'

'This morning.'

'When you went to the office?'

'No, before that.'

'How long before?'

'What, don't you remember?'

'I want to hear you say it.'

'When I got that call and you woke up and went in the kitchen to make coffee. Catarella told me first, but I didn't understand a word of it, then Fazio explained that a girl had disappeared.'

'And what did you do next?'

'I had a shower and got dressed.'

'Oh, no, you didn't, you disgusting hypocrite! You laid me out on the kitchen table! Monster! How could you even think of making love to me when that poor girl—'

'Livia, stop and think for a minute. When I got that call, I had no idea how serious—'

'See? That newsman is right, what's his name, the one who said you're incompetent and don't understand a thing! Actually, no, you're worse! You're a brute! A filthy pig!'

She ran out, and the inspector heard the key turn in the bedroom door. He approached and knocked.

'Come on, Livia. Don't you think you're overdoing it a little?'

'No. You can sleep on the sofa tonight.'

'But it's so uncomfortable! Come on, Livia! I won't sleep a wink!'

No reaction. He decided to play the pity card.

'And I'm sure my wound will start throbbing again!' he said in a pathetic voice.

'Too bad.'

He knew he would never succeed in making her change her mind. He had to resign himself. He cursed under his breath. As if in response, the telephone rang. It was Fazio.

'Didn't I tell you to go home and rest?'

'I couldn't bring myself to leave it all hanging, Chief.'

'What do you want?'

'They just phoned. Inspector Minutolo wanted to know if you could drop by.'

*

He arrived in a flash in front of the locked gate. On the way there, it occurred to him he hadn't told Livia he was going out. Despite their quarrel, he should have. Even if only to avoid another spat. Livia was liable to think he'd gone to spend the night at a hotel out of spite. Too bad.

But now, how was he going to get somebody to open the gate for him? By the light of the headlamps, he could see there was no bell, no intercom, nothing. The only solution was the car horn. He hoped he didn't have to keep honking until he woke up the whole town. He started with a timid, quick toot, and immediately a man came out of the house. Fiddling with the keys, the man opened the gate and Montalbano drove through, pulled up, and got out of the car. The man who'd come out introduced himself.

'I'm Carlo Mistretta.'

The doctor brother was a well-dressed man of about fifty-five, rather short, with fine spectacles, a ruddy face, little facial hair, and a hint of a pot belly. He looked like a bishop in mufti. He continued:

'When your colleague informed me that the kidnappers had called, I came running, because Salvatore felt ill.'

'How is he now?'

'I gave him something I hope will let him sleep.'

'How about his wife?'

The doctor threw his hands up by way of reply.

'Has she still not been informed of the—'

'No,' the doctor said, 'that's the last thing she needs. Salvatore told her Susanna's in Palermo for exams. But my poor sister-in-law is not exactly lucid; she often goes blank for whole hours at a time.'

In the living room there was only Fazio, who'd fallen asleep in the usual armchair, and Fifì Minutolo, sitting in the other armchair, smoking a cigar. The French doors were wide open, letting in cool, penetrating air.

'Were you able to find out where the phone call was made from?' was the first thing Montalbano asked.

'No. It was too brief,' replied Minutolo. 'Now listen up; we can discuss things later.'

'OK.'

As soon as he sensed Montalbano's presence, Fazio, with a kind of animal reflex, opened his eyes and leapt to his feet.

'So you're here, Chief? You want to listen? Sit down here in my place.'

Without waiting for an answer, he turned on the tape recorder.

'Hello? Who is this? This is the Mistretta residence. Who is this?'

. . .

'Who is this?'

'Listen to me and don't interrupt. The girl is here with us, and she's doing all right for now. Recognize her voice?'

. . .

'Papa . . . Papa . . . please . . . help . . .'

. . .

'Did you hear? Get a lot of money ready. I'll call again day after tomorrow.'

. . .

'Hello? Hello? Hello?'

. . .

'Play it over again,' said the inspector.

The last thing he wanted to do was to listen again to the fathomless despair in that girl's voice, but he had to do it. As a precaution, he covered his eyes with one hand, in case his emotions got the better of him.

After the second listening, Dr Mistretta, face buried

in his hands, shoulders heaving with sobs, rushed out, almost running into the garden.

'He's very fond of his niece,' Minutolo commented. Then, looking at Montalbano: 'So?'

'That was a recorded message. Do you agree?'

'Absolutely.'

'The man's voice is disguised.'

'Clearly.'

'And there are at least two of them. Susanna's voice is in the background, a bit far from the recorder. When the man making the recording says, "Recognize her voice?" a few seconds pass before Susanna speaks, the time it takes for his accomplice to lower her gag. Then he gags her again almost immediately, cutting her off in the middle of her plea, which was surely supposed to be "Help *me*." What do you think?'

'I think there may only be one of them. First he says, "Recognize her voice?" then he goes over and removes the gag.'

'That's not possible, because in that case the pause between the kidnapper's question and Susanna's voice would have been longer.'

'OK. You know something?'

'No. You're the expert.'

'They're not following the usual procedure.'

'Explain.'

'Well, what is the usual procedure for a kidnapping? There are the manual labourers – let's call them Group B

– who are given the task of physically carrying out the kidnapping. After which Group B hands the kidnapped person over to Group C, that is, those in charge of hiding her and taking care of her – more grunt work. At this point Group A comes on the scene. These are the ringleaders, the organizers who will demand the ransom. All these transitions take time, and therefore the ransom request is usually not made until a few days after the kidnapping. Whereas, in our case, it took only a few hours.'

'And what does this mean?'

'In my opinion, it means the group that kidnapped Susanna is the same one that is holding her prisoner and demanding the ransom. It might be a family outfit on a low budget. And if they're not professional, that complicates matters and makes it more dangerous for the girl. Follow me?'

'Perfectly.'

'It may also mean they're holding her somewhere not very far away.' He paused, looking pensive. 'On the other hand, it doesn't look like some fly-by-night kidnapping either. In those cases the ransom demand is usually made with the first contact. They have no time to waste.'

'This business of letting us hear Susanna's voice,' said Montalbano, 'is it normal? I don't think—'

'You're right,' said Minutolo. 'It never happens. You only see it in movies. What usually occurs is that if you don't want to pay up, they wait a bit and then make

the victim write a couple of lines to persuade you.
Or they might send you a piece of his ear. That's usually
the only kind of contact they allow between victim and
family.'

'Did you notice how they spoke?'

'How did they speak?'

'In perfect Italian, with no regional inflection.'

'You're right.'

'So what are you going to do now?'

'What do you want me to do? I'm going to call the
commissioner and tell him the news.'

'That phone call has got me confused,' said Montalbano in conclusion.

'Me, too,' Minutolo agreed.

'Tell me something. Why did you let Mistretta talk
to a newsman?'

'To jump-start things, speed up the tempo. I don't
like the idea of a girl so pretty being at the mercy of
people like that for very long.'

'Are you going to tell the media about this phone
call?'

'Not even in my dreams.'

That was all, for the moment. The inspector went up
to Fazio, who had fallen back asleep, and shook his
shoulder.

'Wake up, I'll take you home.'

Fazio put up a feeble resistance.

'Come on. At any rate, they're not going to call back

until day after tomorrow. They told you themselves, didn't they?'

＊

After dropping Fazio off, he headed home. Entering without a sound, he went into the bathroom and then got ready to lie down on the sofa. He was too tired even to curse the saints. As he was taking off his shirt, he noticed, in the dark, that the bedroom door was ajar. Apparently Livia was sorry for having banished him. He went back in the bathroom, finished undressing, tiptoed into the bedroom, and lay down. A short spell later, he stretched out close to Livia, who was in a deep sleep. The minute he closed his eyes he was in dreamland. Then suddenly, *clack*. Time's spring jammed. Without looking at the clock, he knew it was three twenty-seven and forty seconds. How long had he slept? Luckily he fell back asleep almost at once.

Livia woke up around seven the next morning. Montalbano, too. And they made peace.

＊

Francesco Lipari, Susanna's boyfriend, was waiting for him in front of the station. The dark circles under his eyes betrayed his agitation and sleepless nights.

'I'm sorry, Inspector, but early this morning I called Susanna's father and he told me about the phone call, so—'

'What?! I thought Minutolo didn't want anyone to know!'

The kid shrugged.

'All right, come inside. But don't tell anyone at all about that phone call.'

As he went in, the inspector told Catarella he didn't want to be disturbed.

'Is there something you have to tell me?' he asked the young man.

'Nothing in particular. But it occurred to me there was something I forgot to tell you the last time I saw you. I don't know how important it is . . .'

'In this case, everything is potentially important.'

'When I discovered Susanna's motorbike, I didn't go straight to her house to tell her father. I took the unmade road all the way back to Vigàta, then turned around and went back to where I'd started.'

'Why?'

'I dunno. At first it was sort of instinctive. I thought she might have fainted or fallen and lost her memory, so I decided to look for her along that road. Then, on the way back, it wasn't her I was looking for any more, but—'

'The helmet she always wore,' said Montalbano.

The boy looked at him, wide-eyed with surprise.

SIX

'You thought of it, too?'

'Me? Well, when I arrived at the scene, my men had already been there for a while. And when Susanna's father told them she always wore a helmet, they looked for it everywhere, not only along the road but also in the fields beyond the walls.'

'I just can't imagine the kidnappers forcing Susanna in the car with her struggling and screaming with her helmet on.'

'Me neither, as far as that goes.'

'But do you really have no idea how things went?' asked Francesco, torn between incredulity and hope.

The kids of today! thought the inspector. *They put their faith in us so readily, and we do everything we can to disappoint them!*

To prevent Francesco from seeing his emotion (but was this not perhaps a first sign of senility and not an effect of his injury?), he bent down to look at some papers inside a drawer. He didn't answer until he was sure he could speak in a steady voice.

'There are still too many things we can't explain. The first is: why did Susanna take a road she'd never taken before to come home?'

'Maybe there's somebody around there—'

'Nobody knows her. And nobody even saw her pass by on her motorbike. Of course it's possible one of them's not telling the truth. In that case, the person not telling the truth is an accessory to the kidnapping, maybe only as a coordinator. Maybe he was the only one who knew that on that specific day, at that specific hour, Susanna would come down that road. Do you follow?'

'Yes.'

'But if Susanna took that road for no particular reason, then the kidnapping must have resulted from an entirely chance encounter. But that can't be how it went.'

'Why not?'

'Because the kidnappers are showing that they planned the job in advance and are therefore at least minimally organized. We know from the phone call that this was not a rush job. They seem in no hurry to get rid of Susanna. This means they're keeping her in a safe place. And it's unlikely they found such a place in a matter of hours.'

The young man said nothing. He was concentrating so hard on the words he was hearing that the inspector thought he could hear the gears churning in his brain. Francesco then drew his conclusion.

'According to your reasoning, Susanna was very probably kidnapped by someone who knew she was going to take the unmade road that evening. Someone who lives around there. In that case we need to get to the bottom of this, find out everybody's name, verify that—'

'Stop. If you're going to start calculating and forming hypotheses, you must also be able to anticipate failure.'

'I don't understand.'

'I'll explain. Let's assume we conduct a careful investigation of all those who live on that road. We come to know every detail of their lives, down to the number of hairs on their arses, and in the end we learn that there was never any contact whatsoever between Susanna and any of them. Nothing at all. What do you do then? Start over from the top? Give up? Shoot yourself?'

The kid didn't let up.

'Well, what do *you* think one should do?'

'Formulate and test other hypotheses at the same time, letting them all play out simultaneously, without giving preference to any single one, even if it appears to be the most likely to prove true.'

'And have you formed any others?'

'Of course.'

'Could you tell me one?'

'If it'll make you feel better ... OK, Susanna's on that

road because someone told her to meet him or her in that
very place, because there's never anyone around . . .'

'That's not possible.'

'What's not possible? That Susanna might have had
such an appointment? Can you really be so certain? I'm
not saying, mind you, that it was some sort of amorous
rendezvous. Maybe she was meeting someone for reasons
we don't know. So she goes to this appointment unaware
that she's walking into a trap. When she arrives, she parks
the motorbike, removes her helmet, but keeps it in her
hand, knowing that the meeting is supposed to be brief.
Then she approaches the car and is kidnapped. Does that
work for you?'

'No,' Francesco said firmly.

'And why not?'

'Because when we saw each other that afternoon, she
would surely have told me about this prearranged meeting.
I'm sure of it, believe me.'

'I believe you. But maybe Susanna didn't get a chance
to tell you.'

'I don't understand.'

'Did you accompany her on her way to her friend's
house that evening?'

'No.'

'Susanna had a mobile phone, which we haven't found,
right?'

'Right.'

'She could have received a phone call after she left

your place, as she was on her way to her friend's house, and agreed to the meeting only then. And since you haven't seen her since, she had no way of letting you know.'

The boy thought about this for a moment. Then he made up his mind.

'I guess it's possible.'

'So what are you trying to tell me with all these doubts of yours?'

Francesco didn't answer. He buried his face in his hands. Montalbano threw oil on the fire.

'But we may be entirely on the wrong track.'

The kid jumped out of his chair.

'What are you saying?'

'I'm merely saying that it's possible we're starting from a mistaken assumption. That is, that Susanna went home by way of that unmade road.'

'But that's where I found the motorbike!'

'That doesn't necessarily mean Susanna took that road when leaving Vigàta. I'll give you an example, the first thing that comes into my head. Susanna leaves her friend's home and takes the road she normally does. This road is used by many of the people who live in the houses before and after the villa, and it ends a couple of miles past the Mistretta house in a kind of rural suburb of Vigàta — La Cucca, I think it's called. It's a road of commuters, peasants, and others who prefer to live in the country even though they work in Vigàta. They all know one another, and probably go back and forth on that road at the same times of day.'

'Yes, but what has that got to do with—'

'Let me finish. The kidnappers have been following Susanna for some time, to see what kind of traffic there is around the hour she comes home, and to work out where would be the best place for them to make their move. That evening, they get lucky. They can carry out their plan at the intersection with the unmade road. In one way or another, they block Susanna's path. There are at least three of them. Two of them get out of the car and force her to get in. The car drives off, probably taking the unmade road in the direction of Vigàta. One of the two, however, stays behind, grabs the motorbike, and follows the car. Then he leaves the bike at some point along the unmade road. This would explain, among other things, why the motorbike was pointed in the direction of Vigàta. Then he gets in the car with the others, and they drive off into the sunset.'

Francesco looked doubtful.

'But why bother with the motorbike? What do they care? Their main concern is to get out of there as quickly as possible.'

'But I just told you that road's full of commuters! They couldn't just leave the motorbike on the ground. Someone might think there'd been an accident, another might recognize the motorbike as Susanna's ... In short, alarm bells were ringing and they didn't have time to find a good place to hide it. And while they were at it, they might as well move it onto the unmade road, where nobody ever drove by. But we can form other hypotheses as well.'

'We can?'

'As many as you like. After all, we're conducting a lesson here. But first I must ask you a question. You told me you sometimes accompanied Susanna all the way home.'

'Yes.'

'Was the gate open or closed?'

'Closed. Susanna would open it with her key.'

'So we can also hypothesize that Susanna, having leaned her motorbike against the gate, was reaching for her key when somebody came up to her on foot, someone she's seen a few times along that road, some commuter. The man pleads with her to take him on her motorbike to the unmade road, making up some story or other – say, that his wife felt sick in the car on her way to Vigàta and called him on her mobile for help, or that his son got hit by a car ... something like that. Susanna feels she can't refuse, so she has him get on the back of her bike and sets out. And in this case as well, we have an explanation for the positioning of the motorbike. Another possibility—'

Montalbano suddenly broke off.

'Why don't you go on?'

'Because I'm bored. Don't kid yourself: it doesn't matter that much exactly what happened.'

'It doesn't?'

'No, because, if you think about it ... The more we examine the details that seem essential to us, the fuzzier, the more out-of-focus they become. Take you, for example. Didn't you come to me to find out whatever happened to Susanna's helmet?'

'Her helmet? Yes.'

'As you can see, the more our discussion progressed, the more the helmet receded into the background. In fact it became so unimportant that we stopped talking about it. The real question is not the "how", but the "why".'

Francesco was opening his mouth to ask another question when the door burst open and crashed loudly against the wall, sending him flying out of his chair in fear.

'What was that?' he asked.

'My 'and slipped,' Catarella said contritely from the doorway.

'What is it?' Montalbano asked in turn.

'Seeing as how you said you din't wanna be disturbed by any disturbers, I hadda come ax you a question in poisson.'

'Go ahead.'

'Is Mr Zito the newsman one of them that youda call disturbers, an' if he in't, in't he?'

'No, he's no disturbance. Put him on.'

'Hi, Salvo, it's Nicolò. Sorry to interrupt, but I wanted to tell you I just came into my office—'

'What the hell do I care what your work hours are? Tell it to your employer.'

'No, Salvo, this is serious. I just got in and my secretary told me that ... well, it's about that girl who was kidnapped.'

'OK, tell me what she said.'

'No, I'd rather you came here.'

'I'll drop by as soon as I can.'

'No, right now.'

Montalbano hung up, stood up, and shook Francesco's hand.

✻

The Free Channel, the private television station where Nicolò Zito worked, had their studios in an outlying district of Montelusa. As he was driving there in his car, the inspector tried to guess what could have happened that would make his journalist friend so anxious to tell him about it. And he guessed right. Nicolò was waiting for him at the entrance to the building, and as soon as he saw Montalbano's car pull up, he went out to greet him. He looked upset.

'What is it?'

'This morning, right after the secretary came in to work, there was an anonymous phone call. A man asked

91

her if we had the equipment to record a telephone call and she said yes. He told her to get it all ready, because he was going to call back in five minutes. Which he did.'

They went into Nicolò's office. On his desk was a portable but professional-looking tape recorder. The journalist turned it on. As he'd anticipated, Montalbano heard the same recording he'd heard at the Mistretta home, not one word more or less.

'It's scary. That poor girl . . .' said Zito.

Then he asked:

'Did the Mistrettas get this call? Or do the bastards want us to act as go-betweens?'

'They called late last night.'

Zito breathed a sigh of relief.

'Well, I'm glad for that. But then why did they also send it to us?'

'I've got a very good idea why,' said Montalbano. 'The kidnappers want everyone, not just the father, to know that the girl is in their hands. Normally a kidnapper has everything to gain from silence. These guys, however, are doing everything under the sun to make noise. They want the sound of Susanna begging for help to scare as many people as possible.'

'Why?'

'That's the big question.'

'So what do I do now?'

'If you want to play their game, then broadcast the phone call.'

'It's not my job to help criminals.'

'Good for you! I'll make sure to carve those noble words on your tombstone.'

'You're such an idiot,' said Zito, grabbing his crotch.

'Well, then, since you've declared yourself an honourable journalist, you'll call the judge and the commissioner, tell them about the recording, and make it available to them.'

'That's what I'll do.'

'You'd better do it right away.'

'You in some kind of hurry?' asked Zito as he was dialling the commissioner's office.

Montalbano didn't answer.

'I'll wait for you outside,' he said, getting up and going out.

It was a truly gentle morning, with a light, delicate wind blowing. The inspector fired up a cigarette but didn't have time to finish it before the newsman came out.

'Done.'

'What did they tell you?'

'Not to broadcast anything at all. They're sending an officer to come and pick up the cassette.'

'Shall we go back inside?' asked the inspector.

'You want to keep me company?'

'No, I want to see something.'

When they entered the office, Montalbano told Nicolò to turn on the television and tune in to TeleVigàta.

'What do you want to hear from those idiots?'

'Just wait and you'll understand why I was in such a hurry for you to call the commissioner.'

At the bottom of the screen appeared the words:

SPECIAL EDITION OF TELEVIGÀTA NEWS FOLLOWS

'Shit!' said Nicolò. 'They called them, too! And those sleazeballs are going to broadcast it!'

'Isn't that what you expected?'

'No. And you made me lose the scoop!'

'You want to turn back now? Make up your mind: are you an honest or a dishonest journalist?'

'I'm honest, all right, but losing a scoop of one's own free will really hurts!'

The scroll with the announcement disappeared, and the *TeleVigàta News* logo came onto the screen. Then, without any introduction, Mr Mistretta's face appeared. It was a replay of the appeal he'd already made the day after the kidnapping. Then a newsman appeared.

'We rebroadcast the plea of Susanna's father for a specific reason. Now, please listen to the chilling document that was phoned in to our studios this morning.'

Against a backdrop of the Mistretta villa, one heard the telephone call that was made to the Free Channel. Then they cut to the prune face of Pippo Ragonese.

'Let me say straight away that here at TeleVigàta, the editorial staff were terribly torn over whether to broadcast the phone call we'd just received. The anguished and anguishing voice of Susanna Mistretta is not something our consciences can easily bear hearing, living as we do in a civilized society. But your right to the news prevailed. The public's right to know is sacrosanct, and it is our sacrosanct duty as journalists to respect this right. Otherwise we could no longer proudly call ourselves journalists in the public service. We chose to rebroadcast the girl's father's desperate appeal before letting you hear that telephone call. The kidnappers do not realize, or do not want to realize, that their ransom demand can only come to nothing, given the well-known financial straits of the Mistretta family. In this tragic stalemate, our hope resides in the forces of order, particularly in Inspector Minutolo, a man of vast experience, whom we fervently wish a prompt success.'

The first newsman reappeared and said:

'This special edition will be rebroadcast every hour.'

Party's over, time to go home.

A rock-music programme began.

Montalbano never stopped marvelling at the people who worked in television. For example, they show you images of an earthquake with thousands of victims, whole towns swallowed up, small children wounded and crying, bits of human corpses, and then right afterwards they say: 'And now a few beautiful shots of Carnival in Rio.' Colourful floats, happy faces, sambas, arses.

'The bastard and son of a bitch!' said Zito, turning red in the face and kicking a chair.

'Wait, I'll fix him,' said Montalbano.

He quickly dialled a number and then waited a few minutes, the receiver glued to his ear.

'Hello? Montalbano here. The commissioner, please. Yes, thank you. Yes, I'll remain on the line. Yes. Mr Commissioner? Good day. Sorry to bother you, but I'm calling from the offices of the Free Channel. Yes, I know that Nicolò Zito just called you. Of course, he's a responsible citizen and was only doing his duty ... He set aside his interests as a journalist and ... Of course, I'll tell him ... Well, what I wanted to say, sir, was that as I was sitting here, another anonymous call came in.'

Nicolò looked at him, flabbergasted, shaking his hand at him, *a cacocciola*, as if to say: 'What the hell?'

'The same voice as before,' Montalbano continued, still on the phone, 'told him to get ready to record. Except that when they called back five minutes later, not only was there a bad connection and you couldn't understand a thing they said, but the tape recorder didn't work.'

'What kind of bullshit are you feeding him?' Nicolò said under his breath.

'Yes, Mr Commissioner, I'll remain at the scene and wait for them to retry. What's that you say? TeleVigàta has just broadcast the phone call? That's not possible! And they replayed the father's plea? No, I didn't know. But this is unheard of! It can even be considered a crime! They should have turned the tape over to the authorities, not broadcast it on the air! Just as Zito did! You say the judge is looking into what measures can be taken? Good!

Excellent! Oh, sir, something just occurred to me. Only a hunch, mind you. If they just called back the Free Channel, they certainly must have also called back TeleVigàta. And maybe TeleVigàta had more luck and managed to tape the second call ... Which of course they'll deny having received, because they'll want to save it to broadcast at the right moment ... A dirty game, you're absolutely right ... Far be it from me to give you advice, sir, what with all your expertise, but I think a thorough search of the TeleVigàta offices might produce ... yes ... yes ... My humble respects, Mr Commissioner.'

Nicolò looked at him in admiration.

'You're a master showman!'

'You'll see, between the prosecutor's machinations and the commissioner's search, they won't even have time to piss, let alone rebroadcast their special edition!'

They laughed, but then Nicolò turned serious again.

'To hear first the father, then the kidnappers,' he said, 'it sounds like a conversation between deaf people. The father says he hasn't got a cent, and the others tell him to get the money ready. Even if he sells his villa, how much money could they possibly get?'

'Are you of the same opinion as your distinguished colleague Pippo Ragonese?'

'And what would that be?'

'That the kidnapping is the work of inexperienced Third-Worlders who don't realize they have nothing to gain and everything to lose?'

'Not on your life.'

'Maybe the kidnappers don't have a TV and haven't seen the father's appeal.'

'Or maybe...' Nicolò began but then stopped, as if in doubt.

SEVEN

'Or maybe what?' Montalbano prodded.

'I just had an idea, but I'm embarrassed to tell you what it is.'

'I promise you that no matter how stupid it is, it will never leave this room.'

'It's like something out of an American movie. People in town say that up until about five or six years ago, the Mistrettas lived high on the hog. Then they were forced to sell everything. Isn't it possible that the kidnapping was organized by someone who came back to Vigàta after a long absence and was therefore unaware of the Mistretta family's financial situation?'

'Your idea sounds to me more like something out of Totò and Peppino than an American movie. Use your brains! You can't pull off this kind of kidnapping alone, Nicolò! Some accomplice would surely have told your homecoming son of Vigàta that Mistretta could scarcely put bread on the table! By the way, could you tell me how the Mistrettas happened to lose everything?'

'You know, I don't have the slightest idea myself? I believe they were forced to sell everything off, all at once...'

'To sell off what?'

'Land, houses, shops...'

'They were forced, you say? How strange!'

'What's so strange about it?'

'It's as though, six years ago, they urgently needed money to pay, well, a ransom.'

'But there was no kidnapping six years ago.'

'Maybe not. Or maybe nobody knew about it.'

*

Although the judge had taken immediate action, Tele-Vigàta managed to broadcast a replay of the special report before the restraining order went into effect. And this time not only all of Vigàta, but the entire province of Montelusa watched and listened, spellbound. The news had spread by word of mouth with lightning speed. If the kidnappers' intention had been to make everyone aware of the situation, they had fully succeeded.

One hour later, in the place of another rebroadcast of the special report, Pippo Ragonese appeared on the screen with his eyes popping out of his head. In a hoarse voice he said he felt duty-bound to inform everyone that at that moment the television station was being subjected to 'some highly unusual harassment that was clearly an abuse of power, an intimidation tactic, a veritable persecution'. He explained that the recording of the kidnappers' message had been confiscated by court order and that police were presently searching the premises for something, though nobody quite knew what. He concluded by saying that never in a million years would the authorities succeed in throttling the voice of free information as represented by him and TeleVigàta, and that he would keep the public duly informed of any new developments in this 'dire situation'.

＊

Montalbano relished all the confusion he'd caused from Nicolò Zito's office, then went back to the station. He had barely entered when he received a call from Livia.

'Hello, Salvo?'

'Livia! What's wrong?'

When Livia called him at the office, it usually meant that something serious had happened.

'Marta phoned me.'

Marta Gianturco was the wife of an officer with the Harbour Authority and one of Livia's few friends in Vigàta.

'So?'

'She told me to turn on the television immediately and watch the special edition of *TeleVigàta News*, which I did.'

Pause.

'It was terrible ... that poor girl ... her voice was heartbreaking...' she continued, after a moment.

What was there to say?

'Yeah ... I know...' said Montalbano, just to let her know he was listening.

'Then I heard Ragonese say you were searching his offices.'

'Well ... actually...'

'Are you getting anywhere?'

We're sinking fast, he wanted to say. Instead he said:

'We're making progress.'

'Do you suspect Ragonese of having kidnapped the girl?' Livia asked ironically.

'Livia, this is no time for sarcasm. I told you we were making progress.'

'I hope so,' Livia said stormily, in the sort of tone a low, black cloud might have.

And she hung up.

*

So now Livia had taken to making insulting and threatening phone calls. Wasn't it a bit excessive to call them threatening? No, it was not. She was liable to prosecution, in fact. *Come on, stop being such an idiot and get over your anger. There. Are you calm now? Yes? Then call the person you were thinking of calling and forget about Livia.*

'Hello? Dr Carlo Mistretta? Inspector Montalbano here.'

'Any news?'

'No, I'm sorry to say. But I'd like to have a few words with you, Doctor.'

'I'm terribly busy this morning. And this afternoon as well. I've been neglecting my patients a bit, I'm afraid. Could we do it this evening? Yes? All right, let's see, we could meet at my brother's house around—'

'I'm sorry, Doctor, but I would like to speak to you alone.'

'Do you want me to come to the station?'

'No, you needn't bother.'

'OK, then come to my house around eight o'clock this evening. All right? I live on Via ... well, it's too complicated to explain. Let's do this. I'll meet you at the first petrol station on the road to Fela, just outside Vigàta. At eight o'clock.'

The telephone rang again.

'H'lo, Chief? There's some lady wants to talk to you poissonally in poisson. Says iss a poissonal matter.'

'Did she say what her name is?'

'I tink she said GI Joe, Chief.'

What! Mostly out of curiosity to find out what the woman's real name was, he accepted the call.

'Is det you, Signore? This is Adelina Cirrinciò.'

His housekeeper! He hadn't seen her since Livia

arrived. What could have happened? Or maybe she wanted to threaten him, too, with something like: if you don't free that girl within two days, I'm not going to come to your house and cook for you any more. A terrifying prospect, especially as he remembered one of her favourite sayings: *Tilefunu e tiligramma portanu malanna*, or, 'Phone calls and telegrams bring bad news.' Therefore, if she'd picked up the phone, it meant she had something very serious to tell him.

'What is it, Adelì?'

'Signore, I wanna youta know that Pippina's a jess hedda baby.'

Who the hell was Pippina? And why was she telling him she'd just given birth? His housekeeper realized the inspector was drawing a blank.

'Don' you rimimber, Signore? Pippina's my son a Pasquale's wife.'

Adelina had two criminally inclined sons who were constantly in and out of jail, and the inspector had attended the wedding of the younger son, Pasquale. Had nine months already passed? Jesus, how time flew! He grew sullen. For two reasons: one, because old age was drawing closer and closer and, two, because old age brought to mind banal clichés like the one that had just come into his head. But his anger at having had such a commonplace thought cut short the sadness rising up inside him.

'Boy or girl?'

'Boy, signore.'

'My heartfelt congratulations.'

'Wait, signore. Pasquale an' Pippina said they wanna youta be the godfather atta bappetism.'

In short, he'd done them one good turn by attending the wedding, and now they wanted him do them another by becoming the kid's godfather at the baptism.

'And when's the baptism?'

'In about ten days.'

'Gimme a couple of days to think about it, Adelì, OK?'

'OK. And when's a Miss Livia leaving?'

*

He went to his usual trattoria. Livia was already sitting at a table. From afar one could see, from the look she gave him as he sat down, that this was going to be no picnic.

'So, are you getting anywhere?' she attacked.

'Livia, we spoke less than an hour ago!'

'So what? A lot of things can happen in an hour.'

'Does this seem like the proper place to discuss these things?'

'Yes. Because when you come home you never tell me anything about your work. Or would you rather I come to the station to discuss it, Inspector?'

'Livia, we really are doing everything we can. At this

very moment, most of my men, including Mimì and another squad from Montelusa, are scouring the nearby countryside, looking for—'

'And why, while your men are out scouring the countryside, are you quietly sitting here with me in a trattoria?'

'It's what the commissioner wanted.'

'The commissioner wanted you to eat at a trattoria while your men are working hard and that girl's life is a living hell?'

What a pain in the arse!

'Livia, stop breaking my balls!'

'Hiding behind obscenity, eh?'

'Livia, you would make a peerless agent provocateur. The commissioner has divvied up responsibilities. I'm working with Minutolo, who's in charge of the investigation, while Mimì and others keep searching. It's hard work.'

'Poor Mimì!'

Poor everybody, according to Livia. Poor girl, poor Mimì ... The only person unworthy of her pity was him. He pushed away the dish of plain spaghetti *all'aglio e olio*, which he'd been forced to order because Livia was with him. Enzo, the proprietor, came running, concerned.

'What's wrong, Inspector?'

'Nothing, I'm just not very hungry,' he lied.

Livia didn't make a peep and went on eating. In an attempt to lighten the atmosphere and get himself ready to savour the second course he'd ordered — *aiole* in a sauce whose fragrance was wafting out from the kitchen, sending him positive signals — he decided to tell Livia about the phone call from his housekeeper. He set off on the wrong foot.

'Adelina rang me at the office this morning.'

'I see.'

She shot out the words like bullets.

'What's "I see" supposed to mean?'

'It means Adelina rings you at the office, not at home, because at home I might answer instead of you, which would surely leave her traumatized.'

'OK, never mind.'

'No, I'm curious. What did she want?'

'She wants me to be the godfather at the baptism of her grandson, the son of her son Pasquale.'

'And what did you tell her?'

'I asked her to give me a couple of days to think about it. But I have to confess, I'm leaning toward saying yes.'

'You're insane!'

She said it too loudly. Mr Militello, an accountant sitting at the table to their left, stopped his fork in mid-air, mouth hanging open; Dr Piscitello, sitting at the table on their right, choked on the wine he'd just sipped.

'Why?' asked Montalbano, puzzled at her vehement reaction.

'What do you mean, why? Isn't this Pasquale, your

housekeeper's son, a repeat offender? Haven't you arrested him several times yourself?'

'So what? I would be the godfather of a newborn infant who, until proved otherwise, hasn't yet had the time to become a repeat offender like his father.'

'That's not what I'm saying. Do you know what it means to be the godfather at a baby's baptism?'

'I dunno, you hold the baby while the priest——'

Livia shook her forefinger.

'Sorry, darling, but becoming a godfather means taking on specific responsibilities. Didn't you know?'

'No,' Montalbano said sincerely.

'If anything should happen to the father, the godfather is supposed to take his place in all matters concerning the child. He becomes a kind of stand-in for the father.'

'Really?!' said Montalbano, in shock.

'Ask around, if you don't believe me. So, what may happen is that next time you arrest this Pasquale, he'll go to jail and you'll have to see to the needs of his son and keep an eye on his behaviour ... Can you imagine that?'

'Er ... shall I bring the fish?' asked Enzo.

'No,' said Montalbano.

'Yes,' said Livia.

Livia refused to let him drive her home, taking the bus to Marinella instead. Since he hadn't eaten anything, Montalbano skipped the walk along the jetty and went back to the office. It wasn't even three o'clock yet. Catarella intercepted him in the main entrance.

'Ahh, Chief! Chief! The c'mishner called!'

'When?'

'Now, now! In fack, he's still onna line!'

The inspector grabbed the phone from the cupboard that passed for a switchboard.

'Montalbano? You must activate yourself immediately,' Commissioner Bonetti-Alderighi said in an imperious tone.

How was he supposed to do that? By pushing a button? Turning a knob? And wasn't the propellerlike spin his balls went into whenever he so much as heard the commissioner's voice a kind of activation?

'Yes, sir.'

'I've just been informed that Inspector Augello fell and hurt himself in the course of his investigations. He must be immediately replaced. You, for the moment, will take over for him. But don't take any initiatives. Within a few hours I'll arrange for a younger person to step in.'

Ah, how kind and sensitive of the commissioner! A younger person. What, did Bonetti-Alderighi somehow think himself a babe in arms?

'Gallo!'

He put all the pique that was bubbling up inside him into that shout. Gallo appeared in an instant.

'What is it, Chief?'

'Find out where Inspector Augello is. Apparently he's hurt himself. We must go and relieve him at once.'

Gallo turned pale.

'*Matre santa!*' he said.

Why was he so worried about Augello? The inspector tried to console him.

'I don't think it's anything serious, you know. He must have slipped and—'

'I was thinking about myself, Chief.'

'Why, what's wrong?'

'I don't know, Chief, it must've been something I ate ... The fact is that my stomach's all upside down and I'm running to the toilet every couple of minutes.'

'Well, you'll just have to hold it in.'

Gallo went out muttering to himself, then returned a few minutes later.

'Inspector Augello and his team are in Cancello district, on the road to Gallotta. About forty-five minutes from here.'

'Let's go. Go and fetch the patrol car.'

*

They'd been rolling along the provincial road for over half an hour when Gallo turned to Montalbano and said:

'Chief, I can't take it any more.'

'How far are we from Cancello?'

'A couple of miles at most, but I—'

'OK, pull over the first chance you get.'

On their right began a sort of trail marked by a tree with a board nailed to it. On the board were the words

FRESH EGGS. The countryside was uncultivated, a forest of wild plants.

Gallo turned onto the trail, stopped almost at once, dashed out of the car, and disappeared behind a thicket of boxthorn. Montalbano also got out and lit a cigarette. About a hundred yards away was a little white dice of a country cottage with a small garden in front. That must be where the fresh eggs were sold. He walked over to the edge of the trail and started to open the zip on his trousers, but it promptly got stuck on his shirt and refused to budge any further. Montalbano looked down to examine the hitch, and as he was lowering his head, a shaft of light struck him square in the eyes. Once he'd finished, the zip got stuck again, and he repeated the motion, with the same result. That is, he lowered his head and the shaft of light struck his eyes again. He looked to see where the gleam was coming from, and there, half hidden by the bottom part of a bush, was some sort of round object. He immediately realized what it was, and in two strides he was in front of the bush. A motorcycle helmet. Small. Made for a woman's head. It must not have been lying there very long, because there was only a very fine layer of dust on it. New, no scrapes. He pulled a handkerchief out of his pocket, wrapped it around his right hand, fingers included, crouched down, grabbed the helmet, and flipped it over. Then he flopped face-down on the ground to look carefully inside it. It appeared to be very clean. No bloodstains. Two or three long strands of blonde hair were snagged inside it and stood out against the black padding. He was absolutely certain the helmet belonged to Susanna.

'Hey, Chief, where are you?'

It was Gallo. He put the helmet back the way he'd found it and stood up.

'Come here.'

Gallo approached, his curiosity aroused. Montalbano pointed to the helmet.

'I think that's the girl's.'

'You really are one lucky arse,' Gallo couldn't help saying.

'It's your arse that's the lucky one,' said the inspector. 'My compliments to its investigative skills.'

'But if the helmet is here, it means the girl is being held somewhere nearby! Should I call for reinforcements?'

'That's what they want you to think, and that's why they dumped the helmet here. They're trying to throw us off the trail.'

'So what should we do?'

'Get ahold of Augello's team and have them send somebody to stand guard here. Meanwhile, don't you move from this spot until they arrive. I don't want some passerby to find the helmet and make off with it. And move the car as well, because you're blocking the way.'

'Who is ever going to pass this way?'

Montalbano, who had started walking away, didn't answer.

'And where are you going?'

'I'm going to see if they really do have fresh eggs.'

As he approached the cottage, the sound of clucking grew louder and louder, but he didn't see any chickens. The coop must have been behind the house. As he entered the garden, a woman came out of the open front door of the cottage. She was thirtyish, tall, with black hair but fair skin, and a full, beautiful body. She was sort of dressed up and wearing high heels. For a moment Montalbano thought she was a lady who'd come to buy eggs. But the woman smiled at him and said in dialect:

'Why'd you leave your car so far away? You could have parked it right here in the front.'

Montalbano made a vague gesture with his hand.

'Please come in,' said the woman, going in first.

A wall divided the small house's interior into two rooms. The one in front, which must have been the dining room, featured a table in the middle with four baskets of eggs on top, as well as four cane chairs, a sideboard with a phone, a refrigerator, and a small gas stove in the corner. Another corner was hidden by a plastic curtain. The only thing that looked out of place in the room was a small cot that served as a sofa. Everything was sparkling clean. The young woman stared straight at him but said nothing. A few moments later she finally asked, in a whisper the inspector didn't know what to make of:

'Did you come for eggs, or . . . ?'

What was 'or . . .' supposed to mean? The only way to
find out was to see what would happen.

'Or . . .' Montalbano said.

The woman got up, cast a quick glance at the back
room, then closed the door. The inspector imagined there
must be someone, perhaps a sleeping child, in the other
room, obviously the bedroom. The woman sat down on
the cot, took off her shoes, and started unbuttoning her
blouse.

'Close the front door. If you want to wash, you'll find
everything behind the curtain,' she said to Montalbano.

So that was what she'd meant by 'or . . .' He raised his
hand.

'That's OK,' he said.

EIGHT

The woman gave him a puzzled look.

'I'm Inspector Montalbano.'

'*Madonna biniditta!*' she cried, turning red in the face and jumping up like a spring.

'Don't be afraid. Have you got a permit to sell eggs?'

'Yessir. I'll go and get it.'

'That's the important thing. You don't have to show it to me, but I'm sure my colleagues will ask to see it.'

'Why? What happened?'

'First answer me. Do you live here alone?'

'No, with my husband.'

'Where is he now?'

'In there.'

Right there? In the other room? Montalbano's jaw dropped. What? Her husband just sat there, cool as a cucumber, while his wife fucked the first man to walk by?

'Call him.'

'He can't come.'

'Why not?'

'He got no legs. They had to cut 'em off after the accident,' she said.

'What accident?'

'Tractor flipped over when he was ploughing the fields.'

'When did this happen?'

'Three years ago. Two years after we got married.'

'Let me see him.'

The woman went and opened the door, then stood aside. The inspector went in. His nose was immediately assailed by a strong smell of medication. In a large double bed, a man lay half asleep and breathing heavily. In one corner was a television with an armchair in front of it. The top of the dressing table was entirely covered by medicine bottles and syringes.

'They also cut off 'is left hand,' the woman said softly. 'He's in terrible pain, day and night.'

'Why don't you put him in a hospital?'

'Because I can take better care of him. The problem is the medications cost so much and I don't want him to go without 'em. I'd sell my own eyes if I had to. That's why I receive men here. Dr Mistretta told me to give him an injection when the pain gets too bad. Just an hour ago he was crying like a baby, asking me to kill him. He wanted to die. So I gave him an injection.'

Montalbano looked over at the dresser. Morphine.

'Let's go back in the other room.'

They went back in the dining room.

'Do you know that a girl has been kidnapped?'

'Yessir. I seen it on TV.'

'Have you noticed anything unusual around here the last few days?'

'Nothing.'

'Are you sure?'

The woman hesitated.

'The other night ... but it was probably nothing.'

'Tell me anyway.'

'The other night I was lying awake in bed and I heard a car drive up ... I thought maybe it was someone coming to see me, so I got up.'

'You receive clients even at night?'

'Yessir. But they're nice men, respectable, and so they don't want anybody to see 'em during the day. But they always call before they come. That's why I was surprised this car came, 'cause nobody'd called. But then the car pulled up here and turned around, 'cause there's no room anywhere else.'

This poor woman and her wretched, bedridden husband couldn't possibly have anything to do with the kidnapping. Their house, moreover, was out in the open and heavily frequented by outsiders day and night.

'Listen,' said Montalbano, 'near the spot where we left the car, we found something that might belong to the girl who was kidnapped.'

The woman turned white as a sheet.

'We got nothing to do with that,' she said firmly.

'I know. But you're going to be questioned. Tell them about the car, but don't mention that people come to see you at night. And don't let them see you dressed like that. Remove your make-up and those high-heeled shoes. And put the cot in the bedroom. All you sell here is eggs, got that?'

He heard a car and went outside. The patrolman summoned by Gallo had arrived. But with him was also Mimì Augello.

'I was about to come and relieve you,' said Montalbano.

'There's no longer any need,' said Mimì. 'They've already sent Bonolis over to coordinate the search. I guess the commissioner didn't want to put you in charge for even a minute. We can go back to Vigàta.'

While Gallo was showing his colleague where the helmet was, Mimì, with Montalbano's help, climbed into the other car.

'What on earth happened to you?'

'I fell into a ditch full of stones. I must have broken a few ribs. Did you report that you'd found the helmet?'

Montalbano slapped himself on the forehead.

'I forgot!'

Augello knew Montalbano too well not to know that when he forgot to do something, it meant he didn't feel like doing it.

'You want me to call?'

'Yes. Ring Minutolo and tell him what happened.'

*

They had just started driving back when Mimì, with an air of indifference, said:

'You know something?'

'Do you do it on purpose?'

'Do I do what on purpose?'

'Ask me if I know something. That question drives me crazy.'

'OK, OK. About two hours ago, the Carabinieri reported that they'd found the girl's backpack.'

'Are you sure it's hers?'

'Absolutely. Her ID card was inside.'

'Anything else?'

'Nothing. Empty.'

'Good,' said the inspector. 'One to one.'

'I don't get it.'

'First we find one thing, then the Carabinieri find another. Tie game. Where was the backpack?'

'On the road to Montereale. Behind the four-kilometre marker. It was pretty visible.'

'In the very opposite direction from where we found the helmet!'

'Exactly.'

Silence fell.

'Does your "exactly" mean you're thinking exactly the same thing I'm thinking?'

'Exactly.'

'I'll try to translate your brevity into something a little clearer. Namely: all this searching, all this running around, is nothing but a waste of time, one big fuck-up.'

'Exactly.'

'I'll translate some more. The way we see it, the kidnappers, on the night of the kidnapping, got in their car and drove around, throwing various things belonging to Susanna out of the window, to create a variety of phony leads. All of which means—'

'That the girl's not being held anywhere near the places where her things have been found,' Mimì concluded, adding, 'and we're going to have to convince the commissioner of this, otherwise he's liable to have us searching all the way to the Aspromonte.'

*

At the office he found Fazio waiting for him. He already knew about the objects they'd found. He was carrying a small suitcase.

'Going away?'

'No, Chief. I'm going back to the villa. Dr Minutolo wants me to man the phone. I've got a change of clothes in here.'

'Was there something you wanted to tell me?'

'Yessir. After the special edition of *TeleVigàta News*, the phone at the villa started ringing off the hook … Nothing of interest, though. Just interview requests, words of support, people saying prayers, that kind of thing. But there were two that were a little different in tone. The first one was from a former administrative employee at Peruzzo's.'

'What's Peruzzo's?'

'I don't know, Chief. But that's what he called himself. He even said his name didn't matter. And he told me to tell Mr Mistretta that pride may be a good thing, but too much pride is bad. That was all.'

'Hmph. What about the other one?'

'Some old lady. She wanted to talk to Mrs Mistretta. When I finally convinced her Mrs Mistretta couldn't come to the phone, she told me to repeat the following words to her: "Susanna's life is in your hands. Remove the obstacles and take the first step."'

'What do you make of it?'

'Nothing. Chief, I'm leaving. Are you coming by the villa?'

'I don't think so, not tonight. Listen, did you tell Minutolo about these phone calls?'

'No, Chief.'

'Why not?'

'Because I didn't think he would consider them important. Whereas you, I thought, might find them interesting.'

Fazio went out.

Good cop. He'd realized that although those two phone calls might be incomprehensible, they had something in common. Not much, but a sure thing. Indeed, both the former Peruzzo's employee and the old lady were advising Mr and Mrs Mistretta, husband and wife, to change their attitudes. The first advised the husband to be more flexible, while the second suggested that the wife actually take the initiative, by 'removing the obstacles'. Maybe the investigation — which so far had been aimed entirely outwards — needed to change direction. That is, maybe they needed to look inside the kidnap victim's family. At this point it became important to speak with Mrs Mistretta. What sort of condition was she in, anyway? On the other hand, how would he justify his questions if the infirm woman was still unaware that her daughter had been kidnapped? He needed some serious help from Dr Mistretta. He looked at his watch. Twenty minutes to eight.

He phoned Livia to tell her he'd be late for dinner.

'Not once can we eat dinner on time!'

He took it in, didn't react. He didn't have time to squabble with her.

The phone rang again. It was Gallo. They'd decided to keep Mimì in the hospital for observation.

*

The inspector arrived at the first petrol station on the road to Fela at eight p.m. sharp, punctual as a Swiss

watch. No sign, however, of Dr Mistretta. Ten minutes
and two cigarettes later, Montalbano started to worry.
Doctors are never to be trusted. When they give you
an office appointment, they make you wait an hour at
the very least; when they give you an appointment outside the office, they still turn up an hour late, with the
excuse that a patient arrived at the last minute.

Dr Mistretta pulled up next to Montalbano's car in
his four-by-four, only half an hour late.

'Sorry I'm late, but at the last minute, a patient—'

'I understand.'

'Will you please follow me?'

They set out, the one in front and the other behind.
And they went on and on, the one in front and the other
behind, turning off the national road, then off the provincial road, taking unmade road after unmade road and
leaving these behind as well. At last they arrived at an
isolated spot in the open country, pulling up at the gate
to a villa quite a bit bigger than the doctor's geologist
brother's house, and in better condition. It was surrounded
by a high wall. Did these Mistrettas feel somehow dimin-
ished if they didn't live in country villas? The doctor got
out of his car, opened the gate, and drove in, signalling
Montalbano to do the same.

They parked in the garden, which was not as ill-
tended as the other one, but almost.

To the right stood another large, low structure, probably the former stables. The doctor opened the front door

to the villa, turned on the lights, and showed the inspector into a large salon.

'I'll be right back. I have to go and close the gate.'

It was clear he had no family and lived alone. The salon was handsomely furnished and well maintained. One wall was entirely covered by a rich collection of painted glass. Montalbano felt spellbound as he studied the shrill colours and simultaneously naive and refined strokes. Another wall was half covered with tall shelves containing not medical or scientific books, as he would have imagined, but novels.

'Forgive me,' the doctor said upon returning. 'Can I get you something?'

'No, thank you. You're not married, are you, Doctor?'

'No, when I was young I never wanted to get married. Then one day I realized that I was too old to do so.'

'And you live here alone?'

The doctor smiled.

'I know what you mean. This house is too big for only one person. There used to be vineyards and olive groves ... That building you saw next to the house still has wine vats, cellars, and winepresses that nobody uses any more ... And here the upstairs has been closed off since time immemorial. So the answer is yes, I've been living here alone for the last few years. For household matters, I have a maid who works mornings, three days a week. For my meals ... I make do.'

He paused.

'Or else I eat at the house of a lady friend. You would have found out sooner or later, anyway. She's a widow I've been seeing now for over ten years. And there you have it.'

'Thank you, Doctor, but my purpose, in coming to see you, is to learn a little more about your sister-in-law's illness, provided, of course, that you're able and willing—'

'Look, Inspector, there's no professional code of secrecy in this instance. My sister-in-law has been poisoned. The poison's effect is irreversible, and it will inexorably lead to her death.'

'Someone poisoned her?!'

A blow to the head, a stone from the sky, a punch in the face. The sudden, violent shock of this revelation, uttered so placidly, almost without emotion, struck the inspector physically, to the point that his ears made a ringing sound. Or was that short ring actually real? Perhaps the bell of the gate had rung? Or else the telephone on the side table had made a brief *ting*? The doctor, however, gave no sign of having heard anything.

'No need to be so vague,' the doctor said without changing expression, like a teacher pointing out a minor mistake in a student's homework. 'She wasn't poisoned by just "someone", but by one man in particular.'

'And do you know his name?'

'Of course,' he said with a smile.

No, on further inspection it was not a smile that

played on Carlo Mistretta's lips, but rather a smirk. Or more precisely, a sneer.

'Why haven't you reported this?'

'Because there are no legal grounds for prosecution. One can only report it to God in heaven, if one believes in Him. But He, I'm sure, is well aware of the situation.'

Montalbano began to understand.

'So, when you say Mrs Mistretta has been poisoned, you're speaking somewhat metaphorically, I gather?'

'Let's say I'm not sticking to a strictly scientific vocabulary. I'm using words and expressions that, as a doctor, I ought not to use. But you didn't come here for medical advice.'

'And with what has Mrs Mistretta been poisoned?'

'With life. As you see, I keep using words that would be unacceptable in any diagnosis. She's been poisoned by life. Or, better yet: someone has cruelly forced her to enter an obscene realm of existence. And at a certain point, Giulia refused to go any further. She dropped all her defences, all resistance, and gave up the will to live.'

He was well spoken, this Carlo Mistretta. But the inspector needed to hear facts, not well-turned sentences.

'Excuse me, Doctor, but I'm required to ask you more. Was it the husband, perhaps unwittingly, who . . . ?'

Carlo Mistretta's lips parted, uncovering just the edge of his teeth. This, on the other hand, was his manner of smiling.

'My brother? Are you kidding? He would give his

own life for his wife. And when you know the whole story, you'll see that your suspicion was absurd.'

'A lover?'

The doctor looked dazed.

'Eh?'

'I was saying, perhaps another man, some amorous disappointment, if you don't mind my—'

'I believe the only man in Giulia's life has always been my brother.'

At this point Montalbano lost patience. He'd grown fed up with playing charades. On top of this, he wasn't too keen on this Dr Mistretta. He was about to open his mouth to ask more questions when the doctor, as though sensing the inspector's change of mood, raised his hand to stop him.

'A brother,' he said.

Jesus Christ! Now where'd this brother come from? Whose brother?

He'd known from the start that between all the brothers, uncles, in-laws, nephews, and nieces, this case was going to drive him crazy.

'Giulia's brother,' the doctor continued.

'Mrs Mistretta has a brother?'

'Yes. Antonio.'

'And why hasn't he—'

'He hasn't been heard from in the current crisis because he and Giulia haven't spoken for some time. A long time.'

At this point something happened that often happened to Montalbano during the course of an investigation. That is, a variety of apparently unrelated facts all came together at once in his brain, each piece assuming its proper place in the puzzle. And this occurred even before he had full knowledge of them. Thus it was the inspector's own lips, almost entirely of their own will, that said:

'Shall we say six years?'

The doctor looked at him in surprise.

'Do you already know the whole story?'

Montalbano made a gesture that meant nothing.

'No, not six years,' the doctor corrected him, 'but it's true that it all began six years ago. You see, my sister-in-law, Giulia, and her brother, Antonio, who is three years her junior, were orphaned in early childhood. A terrible misfortune. Their parents died in a railway accident. They owned a bit of property. The orphans were taken in by an uncle from the mother's side, a bachelor, who treated them well and with great affection. Giulia and Antonio became very attached as they grew up, as often happens with orphaned siblings. Shortly after Giulia's sixteenth birthday, the uncle died. He had very little money, and so Giulia left school so that Antonio could continue his studies. She took a job as a salesgirl. Salvatore, my brother, met her when she was twenty and fell in love with her. Actually, they both fell in love. But Giulia refused to marry him before Antonio had graduated and found a decent job. She never accepted the least bit of financial help from her future husband. She did everything herself. Finally Antonio became an engineer, found a good job, and Giulia and Salvatore could get married. Three years later, my brother was offered a job in Uruguay. He accepted and went to live there with his wife. Meanwhile—'

The trill of the telephone shattered the silence of the villa and the surrounding countryside like a burst of Kalashnikov fire. The doctor sprang to his feet and went over to the console the phone was on.

'Hello? ... Yes, what is it? ... When? ... Yes, I'll be right over ... Inspector Montalbano's here with me; would you like to speak to him?'

He was pale. He turned around and, without a word, handed the receiver to the inspector. It was Fazio.

'Chief? I tried you at the office and at home, but nobody could tell me where ... Listen, the kidnappers just called, not ten minutes ago ... I think it's better if you come here yourself.'

'I'm on my way.'

'Just a minute,' said Carlo Mistretta. 'I need to get some medication for Salvatore. He's very distraught.'

He went out. They'd phoned sooner than they'd said. Why? Perhaps something had gone wrong for them and they no longer had much time? Or was it simply a tactic to confuse everyone? The doctor returned with a small bag.

'I'll go out first, and you can follow me in your car. There's a short cut to my brother's house from here.'

NINE

They arrived in less than half an hour. A uniformed policeman from Montelusa who didn't know the inspector opened the gate. He let the doctor pass and then blocked Montalbano's car.

'Who are you?'

'What I wouldn't give to know! Let's just say that, conventionally speaking, I'm Inspector Montalbano.'

The policeman gave him a puzzled look, but let him drive through. In the living room they found only Minutolo and Fazio.

'Where is my brother?' the doctor asked.

'Listen,' said Minutolo, 'when listening to the phone call he nearly passed out. So I went upstairs to call the nurse, who roused him and persuaded him to go and lie down.'

'I'm going upstairs,' said the doctor.

And he left, bag in hand. Fazio, meanwhile, had set up the equipment near the telephone.

'This one's also a recorded message,' Minutolo began. 'And this time they get to the point. Listen, and we'll talk afterwards.'

Pay close attention. Susanna's health is fine, but she's feeling desperate because she wishes she could be at her mother's side. Get six billion lire ready. I repeat, six billion lire. The Mistrettas know where to find it. Goodbye.

The same disguised male voice that was in the first recording.

'Did you manage to trace the call?' Montalbano asked.

'You ask such useless questions!' Minutolo retorted.

'This time they didn't let us hear Susanna's voice.'

'Right.'

'And they talk in lire.'

'How did you expect them to talk?' Minutolo asked sarcastically.

'In euros.'

'Isn't it the same thing?'

'No, it's not. Unless you belong to that class of shopkeepers who think a thousand lire's the same as a euro.'

'What's your point?'

'Nothing, just an impression.'

'Say it.'

'The person sending the message still thinks the old way. It comes more naturally to him to count in lire instead of euros. He didn't say "three million euros", he said six billion lire. In short, it seems to me that the man on the phone is of a certain age.'

'Or he's clever enough to have us thinking that way,' said Minutolo. 'He's taking us for a ride the way he did when he scattered the helmet and backpack at the opposite ends of town.'

'Can I go outside for a bit? I need some air,' said Fazio. 'I'll be back in five minutes. In any case, if the phone rings, you're here to pick up.'

Not that he really needed to go out. He just didn't feel right, listening to a conversation between his superiors.

'Go ahead, go ahead,' Minutolo and Montalbano said in unison.

'But there is something new, and rather serious, in my opinion, in that phone call,' Minutolo resumed.

'Right,' said Montalbano. 'The kidnapper is certain that the Mistrettas know where to find six billion lire.'

'Whereas we haven't the slightest idea.'

'But we could.'

'How?'

'By putting ourselves in the kidnappers' shoes.'

'Is this some kind of joke?'

'Not in the least. What I mean is that we, too, could force the Mistrettas to take the necessary steps in the right direction, the one that leads to the possible ransom money. And those steps might clear up a whole lot of things for us.'

'I don't understand.'

'Let me sum it up for you. The kidnappers knew right from the start that the Mistrettas were not in any position to pay a ransom, and yet they kidnapped the girl anyway. Why? Because they also knew that the Mistrettas could, if necessary, get their hands on a large sum of money. Do you agree so far?'

'Yes.'

'Mind you, the kidnappers are not the only ones who know that the Mistrettas can do this.'

'They're not?'

'No.'

'And how do you know?'

'Fazio reported two strange phone calls to me. Have him repeat them to you.'

'And why didn't he report them to me?'

'It must have slipped his mind,' Montalbano lied.

'Concretely speaking, what should I do?'

'Have you informed the judge of this last message?'

'Not yet. I'll do it right now.'

He made as if to lift the receiver.

'Wait. You should suggest to him that, since the kidnappers have now made a specific request, he should put a restraining order on the assets of Mr and Mrs Mistretta, and then report this measure to the press.'

'What would we gain from that? The Mistrettas don't have a cent, and everybody knows it. It would be a pure formality.'

'Of course. It would be a pure formality if it remained

between you, me, the judge, and the Mistrettas. But I said the measure should be made known to the public. Public opinion may be full of shit, as some maintain, but it matters. And the public will begin to wonder if it's true that the Mistrettas know where to find the money, and if so, they'll ask themselves why they don't do what they need to do to get their hands on it. It's possible the kidnappers themselves will have to tell the Mistrettas what they need to do. And something will finally come out in the open. Because, on the face of it, my friend, this doesn't look to me like a simple kidnapping.'

'What is it, then?'

'I don't know. It gives me the impression of a billiards game, where one banks a shot off the cushion in front so that the ball will end up on the opposite side.'

'You know what I say? As soon as he recovers a little, I'm going to put the squeeze on Susanna's father.'

'Go ahead. But keep one thing in mind. Even if, five minutes from now, we learn the truth from the Mistrettas, the judge must still proceed the way we said. With your permission, I'll speak with the doctor as soon as he comes downstairs. I was at his house when Fazio called. He was telling me some interesting things, and I think the conversation is worth continuing.'

At that moment Carlo Mistretta entered the room.

'Is it true they asked for six billion lire?'

'Yes,' said Minutolo.

'My poor niece!' the doctor exclaimed.

'Come, let's get a breath of air,' Montalbano invited him.

The doctor followed him outside as though sleepwalking. They sat down on a bench. Montalbano saw Fazio hurry back into the living room. He was about to open his mouth when the doctor again beat him to it.

'The phone call my brother just described to me relates directly to what I was telling you at my place.'

'I'm sure it does,' said the inspector. 'I think, therefore, that if you feel up to it, you need to—'

'I feel up to it. Where were we?'

'Your brother and his wife had just moved to Uruguay.'

'Oh, yes. Less than a year later, Giulia wrote a long letter to Antonio, suggesting he come and join them in Uruguay. The work prospects were excellent, the country was growing fast, and Salvatore had won the esteem of many important people and was in a position to help him ... I forgot to mention that Antonio had got a degree in civil engineering – you know, bridges, viaducts, roads ... Well, he accepted and came. In the early going, my sister-in-law supported him unstintingly. He remained in Uruguay for five years. Just think, they'd bought two apartments in the same building in Montevideo so they could be close to one another. Among other things, Salvatore sometimes had to leave home for months at a time for work, and he felt reassured to know that he wasn't leaving his young wife alone. Anyway, to cut a long story short, during those five years, Antonio made a fortune. Not so much as an engineer, the way my brother tells it, but through his skill in manipulating the various "free zones" that were so numerous over there ... which was a more or less legal way of evading taxes.'

'Why did he leave?'

'He said he was terribly homesick for Sicily. And he couldn't stand being away any longer. And that, with all the money he now had, he could start up his own business over here. My brother later suspected, though not at the time, that there was a more serious reason.'

'What was that?'

'That maybe he'd made a wrong move and feared for his life. In the two months prior to his departure, his moods had become impossible, though Giulia and Salvatore attributed this to the fact that he was leaving soon. They were like a single family. And Giulia, in fact, suffered a great deal when her brother left. So much, in fact, that Salvatore accepted an offer to go and work in Brazil just so that she could live in a new and different environment.'

'And they didn't see each other again until—'

'Are you kidding? Aside from the fact that they continually called and wrote to each other, Giulia and Salvatore came to Italy at least once every two years and spent their holidays with Antonio. Just think, when Susanna was born...' At the mention of her name, the doctor's voice cracked. 'When Susanna was born rather late in their marriage – they'd given up hope of having children — they brought the baby here so she could be baptized by Antonio, who was too busy to travel. Eight years ago, my brother and Giulia finally moved back. They were tired. They'd been all over South America and they wanted Susanna to grow up in Italy. On top of this, Salvatore had managed to put aside a good deal of money.'

'Could you say he was a rich man?'

'Frankly, yes. And it was I who took care of everything. I invested his savings in stocks, land, property ... As soon as they arrived, Antonio announced that he was engaged and would soon be married. The news took Giulia entirely by surprise. Why hadn't her brother ever mentioned having a girlfriend he intended to marry? She had her answer when Antonio introduced Valeria, his future wife, to her. A beautiful child, barely twenty years old. Antonio, by this point, was pushing fifty, and he fell head over heels for the girl.'

'Are they still married?' Montalbano asked with involuntary malice.

'Yes. But Antonio quickly discovered that to hold on to her, he had to cover her in gifts and fulfil her every desire.'

'Did he ruin himself?'

'No, that's not what happened. "Operation Clean Hands" happened.'

'Wait a minute,' Montalbano interrupted. 'Operation Clean Hands started in Milan over ten years ago, when your brother and his wife were still abroad. And before Antonio got married.'

'True. But you know how things go in Italy, don't you? Everything that happens up north – Fascism, liberation, industrialization – takes a long time to reach us. Like a long, lazy wave. Anyway, a few magistrates finally woke up down here as well. And Antonio had won quite a few government contracts. Don't ask me how, because I don't know and I don't want to know, though it's not hard to imagine.'

'Was he investigated?'

'He made the first move himself. He's a very clever man. To save himself from an eventual investigation that would surely have led to his arrest and conviction, he needed to make some papers disappear. He confessed this, in tears, to his sister, one evening six years ago. And he added that the operation would cost him two billion lire, which he needed to find in a month's time, because he didn't have the cash at that moment and didn't want to borrow from the banks. Those were days when anything he did could be interpreted the wrong way. He said the whole thing almost made him laugh – or cry – because two billion lire was a trifle compared to the huge sums that often passed through his hands. And yet those two billion lire represented his salvation. And they would, of course, be only a loan. He pledged to repay the entire sum within three months, supplemented by any losses incurred by the hasty sell-off. Giulia and my brother stayed up an entire night discussing this. Salvatore would have given the shirt off his back to keep his wife from despairing. The following morning they phoned me and told me of Antonio's request.'

'And what did you do?'

'I must confess that I reacted badly at first. Then I had an idea.'

'What?'

'I said the request seemed senseless, insane, to me. All he needed was to have Valeria sell her Ferrari, her boat, and some jewellery, and they would have their two billion quite easily. Or, if he had trouble reaching that figure, Giulia and Salvatore could make up the difference. But only the difference. In short, I was trying to limit the damage.'

'Did you succeed?'

'No. That same day, Giulia and Salvatore spoke to Antonio and told him about my offer. But Antonio started crying. During that period tears came easily to him. He said that if he accepted, not only would he lose Valeria, but word would get around and he would lose his good standing in the community. People would start saying he was on the verge of bankruptcy. And so my brother decided to sell everything.'

'How much did they get for it, out of curiosity?'

'One billion seven hundred and fifty million lire. By the end of the month they no longer had anything, just Salvatore's pension.'

'Another thing, also out of curiosity, sorry. Do you know how Antonio reacted, when he was given less than the sum he'd asked for?'

'But he got the two billion he'd asked for!'

'Who made up the difference?'

'Do I really have to say?'

'Yes.'

'I did,' the doctor said reluctantly.

'And what happened next?'

'After the three months had gone by, Giulia asked her brother if he could pay back the loan, at least in part. Antonio asked her if they could delay it a week. Mind you, they had nothing in writing: no agreements, no promissory notes, nothing. The only document was a receipt for the two hundred and fifty million lire my brother had insisted on giving me. Four days later, Antonio was indicted for a variety of things, including corruption of a public official, fraudulent balance sheets, and so on. After five months had passed, Giulia, who'd been wanting to send Susanna to an exclusive boarding school in Florence, asked again for some of the money back, only to have Antonio reply rudely that this was not the right time for it. And so Susanna stayed here to study. Well, in short, the right time never came.'

'Are you telling me those two billion lire were never repaid?'

'Precisely. Antonio got off at his trial, quite probably because he'd managed to get rid of the incriminating documents, but one of his businesses mysteriously went bankrupt. Then, by some sort of domino effect, his other businesses all met the same end. Everybody got screwed: creditors, suppliers, employees, everyone. What's more, his wife caught the gambling bug and lost incredible sums of cash. Then, three years ago, Giulia and Antonio had a terrible row, after which they stopped speaking to one another. That was when Giulia first became ill. She no longer wanted to live. And, as I'm sure you understand, it wasn't simply a matter of money.'

'How's Antonio's business doing now?'

'Splendidly. Two years ago he got his hands on some new capital. Personally, I think the bankruptcies were all staged, and in reality he illegally transferred his money abroad. Then, with the new law, he brought it back in, paid his percentage, and put his affairs in order – like all the other crooks who did the same thing, once the law legalized what had once been illegal. Now, because of the earlier bankruptcies, all his businesses are in his wife's name. As for us, I repeat: we haven't seen a cent.'

'What's Antonio's surname?'

'Peruzzo. Antonio Peruzzo.'

Montalbano knew that name. Fazio had mentioned it when reporting the phone call from a former 'administrative employee at Peruzzo's' who'd wanted to remind Susanna's father that too much pride was a bad thing. It was all starting to make sense.

'You do realize,' the doctor went on, 'that Giulia's illness complicates the present situation.'

'In what way?'

'A mother is always a mother.'

'Whereas a father is only sometimes a father?' the inspector retorted brusquely, feeling slightly irritated by the cliché.

'I meant that with Susanna's life in danger, if Giulia weren't so ill, she wouldn't have hesistated for a second to ask Antonio for help.'

'And you think your brother won't?'

'Salvatore has a lot of pride.'

The same word the former Peruzzo employee used.

'So you think there's no way he would ever give in?'

'My God, "no way", I can't say. Maybe, if put under enough pressure . . .'

'Like receiving one of his daughter's ears in the post?'

He'd said it on purpose. The whole manner in which the doctor had set about telling the story had put his nerves on edge. The man acted like he had nothing to do with any of it, even though he'd personally thrown in two hundred and fifty million lire. He only got upset when Susanna's name was mentioned. This time, however, the doctor gave such a start that Montalbano could feel it in the bench they were sitting on, which shook a little.

'Would they go so far?'

'They could go even farther than that, if they want.'

He'd succeeded in rousing the doctor. In the wan light

filtering out from the living room's French doors, he saw him reach into his pocket, pull out a handkerchief, and wipe his brow. What he needed to do now was to prise open the chink he'd opened in Carlo Mistretta's armour.

'I'm going to tell it to you straight, Doctor. The way things stand right now, we haven't the slightest idea who the kidnappers are or where they're keeping Susanna prisoner. Not even a vague idea, despite the fact that we've found your niece's helmet and backpack. Did you know we'd found them?'

'No, this is the first I've heard of it.'

A long, deep silence ensued. Because Montalbano was waiting for the doctor to ask a question. A natural question that any other person would have asked. The doctor, however, didn't open his mouth. So the inspector decided to go on.

'If your brother doesn't take the initiative, the kidnappers could take that as a sign that he's not willing to cooperate.'

'What can we do?'

'Try to persuade your brother to make some overture to Antonio.'

'That won't be easy.'

'Tell him that otherwise you'll have to make the overture yourself. Or is it too hard for you, too?'

'Well, yes, it's very difficult for me too, you know. But certainly not as hard as it is for Salvatore.'

He stood up stiffly.

'Shall we go back inside?'

'I think I'd like to get a little more air.'

'Well, I'm going in. I'll go and see how Giulia's doing, and if Salvatore's awake, which I doubt, I'll tell him what you said to me. If not, I'll tell him tomorrow morning. Good night.'

Montalbano didn't have the time to finish a cigarette before he saw the doctor's silhouette come out of the living room, slip into his car, and drive off.

Apparently Salvatore hadn't been awake and the doctor hadn't been able to talk to him.

The inspector got up and went into the house. Fazio was reading a newspaper, Minutolo had his head buried in a novel, and the uniformed policeman was looking at a travel magazine.

'Sorry to disrupt the quiet contemplation of your reading group,' said Montalbano. Then, turning to Minutolo, 'I need to talk to you.'

They withdrew into a corner of the room, and the inspector told him everything he'd learned from the doctor.

*

While driving home, he glanced at his watch. Christ, it was late! Surely Livia'd already gone to bed. So much the better, because if she was still up, the usual squabble, sure as death, was bound to break out. He opened the door gently. The house was dark, but the outside light on the veranda was on. And there was Livia, in a heavy sweater, sitting on the bench in front of half a glass of wine.

Montalbano bent down to kiss her.

'Forgive me.'

She returned his kiss. The inspector heard singing in his head. There would be no quarrel tonight. Livia, however, seemed melancholy.

'Did you stay up waiting for me?'

'No. Beba called and told me Mimì was in the hospital. So I went to see him.'

TEN

A sudden pang of jealousy. Absurd, of course, but he couldn't help it. Could Livia be melancholy because Mimì lay in a hospital bed?

'How is he?'

'He's got two broken ribs. They're discharging him tomorrow. He'll have to take care of himself at home.'

'Have you eaten?'

'Yes, I couldn't wait any longer,' said Livia, getting up.

'Where are you going?'

'I'm going to warm up some—'

'No, that's all right. I'll get some stuff from the fridge.'

He returned with a dish covered with green and black olives and Ragusan *caciocavallo*. In his other hand, a glass and a bottle of wine. The bread he'd slipped under his arm. He sat down. Livia gazed at the sea.

'I can't stop thinking about that girl who was kidnapped,' she said without turning, 'and something you said to me the first time we talked about it.'

In a way, Montalbano felt reassured. Livia's melancholy was not for Mimì but for Susanna.

'What did I say?'

'That the day she was kidnapped, she went to her boyfriend's apartment to make love.'

'So?'

'But you told me that normally it was always the boy who had to ask; whereas that day, Susanna herself took the initiative.'

'What does that mean, in your opinion?'

'That maybe she had a premonition of what was going to happen.'

Montalbano said nothing. He didn't believe in premonitions, prophetic dreams, or things of that nature.

After a brief silence, Livia asked:

'Are you getting anywhere?'

'Just two hours ago, I had neither compass nor sextant.'

'And now you've got both?'

'That's what I'm hoping.'

He began telling her what he'd learned. When he'd finished speaking, Livia looked puzzled.

'I really don't see what conclusions you can draw from the story this Dr Mistretta told you.'

'No conclusions at all, Livia. But it provides many starting points, many indications that I didn't have before.'

'Such as?'

'Such as the fact – and I'm convinced of this – that they wanted to kidnap not the daughter of Salvatore Mistretta but the niece of Antonio Peruzzo. He's the one with the money. And there's no saying she was kidnapped only for the ransom money; there's also the revenge motive. When Peruzzo went bankrupt, he must have messed up many people's lives. And the kidnappers' strategy is to drag Antonio Peruzzo slowly into the middle of this. Slowly, so that nobody realizes that they wanted to get to him from the start. Whoever organized this kidnapping knew what had happened between Antonio and his sister; they knew that Antonio was beholden to the Mistrettas, and that, as Susanna's godfather, he was responsible . . .'

He trailed off, wanting to bite his tongue. Livia cast a placid glance at him; she looked like an angel.

'Why don't you continue? Did you suddenly remember that you yourself want to become the godfather at the baptism of a criminal's son, and that you may soon have some serious responsibilities of your own?'

'Can we please drop that subject?'

'No, I think we should explore it.'

They explored it, squabbled, made peace, and went to bed.

At three twenty-seven and forty seconds, time's mechanism jammed again. But this time the *clack* sounded far away, and only half woke him up.

*

It was as if the inspector had spoken to crows. (Indeed, people in Vigàta and environs believe that to those who can understand them, these black birds, garrulous creatures that they are, communicate the latest news on the doings of human beings, since they have a clear view – a bird's-eye view, in fact – of the whole.) What happened was that around ten o'clock the following morning, when Montalbano was in his office, the bomb exploded. Minutolo called.

'Do you know what's up at TeleVigàta?'

'No. Why?'

'They've interrupted all their programming. There's only a notice saying that in ten minutes there's going to be a special edition of the news.'

'I guess they're acquiring a taste for it.'

He hung up and rang Nicolò Zito.

'What's this business about a special news broadcast at TeleVigàta?'

'I don't know anything about it.'

'Have the kidnappers got back in touch with you?'

'No. But since we gave them no satisfaction last time . . .'

The inspector went to the cafe near the station. The television was on, displaying a notice for the upcoming broadcast. Some thirty people had gathered round, also awaiting the special edition. Apparently word had spread fast. The notice then disappeared, and the *TeleVigàta News* logo appeared, with the words SPECIAL EDITION underneath. When all this disappeared, the chicken-arse face of Pippo Ragonese appeared.

'Dear viewers, about an hour ago, in the morning post, our editorial offices received a perfectly normal-looking envelope, posted in Vigàta, with no return address, and with our address written in block letters. Inside was a Polaroid snapshot of Susanna Mistretta, who is being held prisoner. We cannot show it to you because we had it sent immediately to the magistrate conducting the investigation, as it was our legal duty to do. On the other hand, we believe it is our journalistic duty to inform you of this development. Susanna is shown at the bottom of some sort of dry well, wearing a heavy chain around her ankle. She is neither blindfolded nor gagged. She is sitting on the ground, atop some rags, her arms around her knees, and looking up with tears in her eyes. On the back of the photo, also in block letters, are the enigmatic words: "*To the person concerned.*"'

He paused, and the camera zoomed in on him. A very close close-up. Montalbano had the distinct impression that at any moment a nice warm egg might come out of Ragonese's mouth.

'The instant we first learned of the girl's kidnapping, our hard-working editorial staff sprang into action. What point was there, we asked ourselves, in kidnapping a girl whose family is in no way able to pay any ransom? Thus we immediately steered our investigation in what turned out to be the right direction.'

Like hell you did, idiot! Montalbano said to himself. *You immediately fingered the immigrants!*

'And today we've come up with a name,' Ragonese continued, his voice sounding like something out of a horror film. 'The name of the person who is in a position to pay the ransom demanded. He is not the girl's father, but perhaps her godfather. The words on the back of the photo, *To the person concerned*, are addressed to him. Out of our longstanding and continuous respect for privacy, we won't mention his name. But we implore him to intervene, as he can and must, without any further delay.'

Ragonese's face disappeared, and a hush came over the cafe. Montalbano left and returned to his office. The kidnappers had got what they wanted. He'd barely sat down when Minutolo called again.

'Montalbano? The judge just sent me the photo that idiot was talking about. Do you want to see it?'

*

Minutolo was alone in the villa's living room.

'Where's Fazio?'

'He went into town. He had to go and sign something for some bank account of his,' Minutolo replied, handing him the photo.

'Where's the envelope?'

'Forensics kept it.'

The photo looked a bit different from the way Ragonese had described it. First of all, it was obvious she was not in a well, but in some sort of cement vat or cistern a good ten feet deep. It clearly hadn't been used for a long time, because on the left-hand side there was a long crack that started at the very top and ran about a foot and half downward, growing wider at the end.

Susanna was in the position he'd described, but she wasn't crying. On the contrary. In her expression Montalbano noticed a determination even stronger than he'd seen in the other photo. She was sitting not on rags, but on an old mattress. And there was no chain around her ankle. Ragonese had made it up, no doubt to add colour. In any case, never in a million years could the girl escape on her own. Beside her, but almost outside the frame, were a dish and a plastic glass. She was wearing the clothes she'd had on when she was abducted.

'Has her father seen this?'

'Are you kidding? Not only have I not let him see the photo, I haven't let him watch TV. I told the nurse not to let him out of his room.'

'Did you inform the uncle?'

'Yes, but he said he couldn't come for another two hours.'

As he asked his questions, the inspector kept looking at the photograph.

'They're probably keeping her in a rainwater cistern that's no longer in use,' said Minutolo.

'Out in the country?'

'Well, yes. They probably used to have these kinds of

tanks here in town, but now I don't think it's very likely. Anyway, she's not gagged. She could scream if she wanted to. If she was in some inhabited area, people would hear her.'

'She's also not wearing a blindfold, for that matter.'

'That doesn't mean anything, Salvo. They could put on ski masks when they visit her.'

'They must have used a ladder to put her down there,' said Montalbano. 'Which they lower whenever she needs to come up. And they probably feed her by lowering a basket on a rope.'

'If we're in agreement, then,' said Minutolo, 'I'll ask the commissioner to intensify the searches across the countryside. Especially around farmhouses. The photo, at least, was good for one thing: we know now she's not being held in a cave.'

Montalbano was about to hand back the photograph, but changed his mind and continued to study it carefully.

'Something not look right to you?'

'The light,' replied Montalbano.

'They probably just put a lamp down there.'

'OK. But not just any lamp.'

'You're not going to tell me they used a floodlight!'

'No. They used one of those lights that mechanics use ... You know, when they need to look at a motor in a garage ... One of those with a long cord ... See these regular lines of shadow that intersect? They're a projection of the broad-mesh screen that protects the lightbulb.'

'And so?'

'But that's not the light that doesn't look right to me. There must be some other light source, because it's casting a shadow on the rim across from it. See? The person taking the photo is not standing on the edge, but beside it, and he's leaning forward to take the shot of Susanna below. This means that the sides of the cistern are quite thick and slightly above ground level. To cast this sort of shadow, the man taking the snapshot must have some kind of light behind him. But, mind you, if it was an intense light, the shadow would be deeper and more sharply defined.'

'I don't see what you're getting at.'

'There was an open window behind the photographer.'

'So?'

'So does it seem logical to you for them to photograph a kidnapped girl with the window open and not put a gag on her?'

'But that merely confirms my hypothesis! They're holding her at some godforsaken country farmhouse, and she can scream all she wants! Nobody will hear her, even with all the windows open!'

'Bah,' said Montalbano, flipping the photo over.

TO THE PERSON CONCERNED

Written in block letters with a ballpoint pen by someone clearly accustomed to writing in Italian. Still, there was something odd, something forced, about the handwriting.

'I also noticed,' said Minutolo. 'He didn't try to falsify his handwriting. It looks rather like somebody left-handed trying to write with his right hand.'

'To me it looks like it was written slowly.'

'What do you mean?'

'I can't really explain it. It's as though somebody with bad, almost illegible handwriting had forced himself to trace every letter clearly, and thus had to slow down his normal writing speed. Then there's another thing. The letter T beginning the word *the* is written over something, as if to correct it. One can clearly see that a W was written there first. He'd probably intended to write "To whom it may concern," then changed it to "To the person concerned". Which is more precise. The person who kidnapped Susanna or masterminded the operation is not just any old thug but someone who understands the importance of words.'

'You really are very good,' said Minutolo. 'But as things stand now, where do your deductions lead us?'

'As things stand now, nowhere.'

'Then shall we try to think about what we need to do? In my opinion, the first thing is to get in touch with Antonio Peruzzo. Do you agree?'

'Absolutely. Have you got his number?'

'Yes. While I was waiting for you, I did a little research. At present Peruzzo has three or four businesses that are subsidiary to a kind of central office in Vigàta, called Progresso Italia.'

Montalbano sneered.

'What's wrong?'

'How could it be otherwise? In perfect keeping with the times. Italy's progress is in the hands of a crook!'

'You're wrong, because officially everything's in his wife's name, Valeria Cusumano. Although I'm convinced the lady has never set foot in that office.'

'OK, call him up.'

'No, you call him. Set up an appointment and go and talk to him. Here's the number.'

The scrap of paper Minutolo handed him had four phone numbers on it. The inspector chose to dial the one for 'Senior Management'.

'Hello? This is Inspector Montalbano. I need to speak with Antonio Peruzzo.'

'Mr Peruzzo's out.'

Montalbano felt his nerves begin to fray.

'Out of the office? Out of town? Out of his mind? Out of—'

'Out of town,' the secretary cut him off coldly, sounding a bit miffed.

'When will he be back?'

'I wouldn't know.'

'Where did he go?'

'To Palermo.'

'Do you know where he's staying?'

'At the Excelsior.'

'Has he got a mobile phone?'

'Yes.'

'Please give me the number.'

'I really don't know if—'

'OK, you know what I'm going to do?' Montalbano said in the sinister tone of someone unsheathing a dagger in the shadows. 'I'm going to go there and ask him for it myself.'

'No! OK, here it is.'

He wrote it down and phoned the hotel.

'I'm sorry, Mr Peruzzo is not in his room.'

'Do you know when he'll be back?'

'Actually, he wasn't even here last night.'

The mobile phone was turned off.

'Well, what do we do now?' asked Minutolo.

'We jerk off big-time,' said Montalbano, still on edge.

At that moment Fazio appeared.

'The whole town's abuzz with rumours! Everybody's talking about Engineer Peruzzo, the girl's uncle. Even though they didn't say his name on TV, everyone knew they meant him. Two factions have formed; one group says the engineer has got to pay the ransom, and the other says he's under no obligation to his niece. But the first group's a lot bigger. They almost came to blows at the Cafe Castiglione.'

'Well, they've managed to screw Peruzzo,' was Montalbano's comment.

'I'm going to have the phones bugged,' said Minutolo.

✻

It didn't take long for the rain falling from heaven onto Antonio Peruzzo to turn into the Great Flood. And this time, the engineer hadn't had enough time to build himself an ark.

*

To all the faithful who went to the church to ask him his opinion, Father Stanzillà, the oldest and wisest priest in town, said there was no doubt about it, human or divine: the uncle must pay the ransom, since he was made the child's godfather at her baptism. Moreover, by shelling out the money the kidnappers were asking for he would only be repaying the girl's mother and father the huge sum he had prised away from them by deceit. And the priest told everyone about the two-billion-lire loan, a matter he knew all about, down to its finest details. In short, he added a good dose of fuel to the fire. It was a good thing for Montalbano that Livia didn't have any churchgoing girlfriends who could tell her what Father Stanzillà thought of the whole affair.

*

On the *Free Channel News*, Nicolò Zito announced to one and all that Antonio Peruzzo, in the face of this specific obligation, was suddenly nowhere to be found. Once again, the engineer had behaved true to form. This flight from a life-and-death matter, however, not only did not absolve him of his responsibility, it made it weigh all the more heavily upon him.

*

On TeleVigàta, Pippo Ragonese proclaimed that since Peruzzo was a victim of the communist judiciary who had managed to remake his fortune thanks to the new government's initiatives to spur private enterprise, it was his moral duty to show that the confidence the banks and institutions had placed in him was well founded. Especially since rumour had it – and it was certainly no secret – that he was considering running for public office among the ranks of those currently renovating Italy. Any gesture that could be interpreted as a rejection of public opinion on his part could have fatal consequences for his political aspirations.

*

Titomanlio Giarrizzo, venerable former presiding judge of the Court of Montelusa, declared in an unwavering voice to his associates at the local chess club that if the kidnappers had appeared before his bench, he would have condemned them to the harshest of punishments but also praised them for having exposed the true face of that notorious scallywag, 'Engineer' Antonio Peruzzo.

*

And Signora Concetta Pizzicato, who had a stand at the fish market with a sign that read CONCETTA THE CLAIR-VOYANT FORTUNE-TELLER'S LIVE FISH, replied to any and all who asked if Peruzzo would pay the ransom: '*Cu al sangu sò fa mali / mori mangiatu da li maiali*,' or 'He who harms his own flesh and blood / shall be eaten by pigs and die.'

*

'Hello? Progresso Italia? This is Inspector Montalbano. Have you heard from Engineer Peruzzo, by any chance?'

'No. No news.'

It was the same girl as before, except that now there was a shrill, almost hysterical tone to her voice.

'I'll call back.'

'No, please, look, it's useless. Mr Nicotra has ordered all telephones to be cut off in ten minutes.'

'Why?'

'We're getting dozens and dozens of calls ... full of insults ... obscenities.'

The girl was about to burst into tears.

ELEVEN

Around five in the afternoon Gallo reported to Montalbano that a nasty rumour had spread about town which, if there was still any need, turned everyone against Antonio Peruzzo. The gossip had it that the engineer, to get out of paying the ransom, had asked a judge to freeze his assets. And that the judge had refused. The story didn't seem to hold water, but the inspector decided to check it out anyway.

'Minutolo? Montalbano here. Do you know, by any chance, what the judge intends to do about Peruzzo?'

'Look, he just called me up and was beside himself. Somebody told him there was a rumour—'

'I've already heard.'

'Well, he told me he's had no contact of any sort, either direct or indirect, with Peruzzo. And that, for the moment, at least, he's not authorized to freeze the assets of any of the Mistrettas' family, friends, acquaintances, or neighbours ... He went on and on, like a river bursting its banks.'

'Listen, have you still got Susanna's photo?'

'Yes.'

'Could you lend it to me till tomorrow? I want to have a better look at it. I'll send Gallo for it.'

'Still fixated on that business about the light?'

'Yes.'

It was a lie. The point wasn't the light, but the shadow.

'OK, Montalbano, but don't lose it. I mean it. Otherwise, who's going to deal with the judge?'

*

'Here's the photo,' said Gallo half an hour later, handing him an envelope.

'Thanks. Send Catarella in here.'

Catarella arrived in a flash, tongue hanging out, like a dog responding to his master's whistle.

'Your orders, Chief!'

'Listen, Cat, that trusty friend of yours ... the guy who's really good with photographs and can blow them up ... what's his name?'

'His name's Cicco De Cicco his name is, Chief.'

'Is he still at Montelusa Central?'

'Yessir, Chief. Still posted at his post.'

'Excellent. Have Imbrò man the switchboard and go

and take this photo to him. Let me explain exactly what I want him to do.'

*

'There's some kid wants to talk to you. His name's Francesco Lipari.'

'Let him in.'

Francesco had lost weight. The dark circles under his eyes now took up half his face. He looked like the Masked Man of comic-book fame.

'Have you seen the photo?' he asked without saying hello.

'Yes.'

'How is she?'

'Look, to begin with, she wasn't in chains, as that idiot Ragonese claimed. And she's not in a well, but inside an empty cistern at least ten feet deep. Given the circumstances, she looked like she was doing all right.'

'Could I see the picture?'

'If you'd come earlier ... I just sent it to Montelusa for an analysis.'

'What kind of analysis?'

He couldn't very well tell Francesco everything he had in mind.

'It's not about Susanna, but the place where they're keeping her.'

'Can you tell if ... if they've hurt her?'

'I really don't think so.'

'Could you see her face?'

'Of course.'

'How did her eyes look?'

This kid was going to make a really good cop.

'She wasn't scared. That's probably the first thing I noticed. In fact, her expression looked very...'

'Determined?' said Francesco Lipari.

'Exactly.'

'I know her. It means she's not giving in to her situation, and that sooner or later she's going to try to escape. The kidnappers will have to watch her very closely.' He paused. Then he asked: 'Do you think Peruzzo will pay up?'

'The way things are going, he's got no choice but to cough up the money.'

'Did you know that Susanna never said anything to me about this business between her mother and her uncle? I felt sort of bad when I heard about it.'

'Why?'

'Because I felt like she couldn't confide in me.'

*

When Francesco left the office, feeling a little more relieved than when he'd entered, Montalbano sat there thinking about what the kid had just told him. There was no question that Susanna was courageous, and her look in the photo confirmed this. Courageous and resolved.

Then why had her voice sounded so desperate when she asked for help in that first phone call? Was there not a contradiction between the voice and the image? Perhaps only an apparent contradiction. The telephone recording was probably made only a few hours after she'd been kidnapped, when Susanna hadn't yet regained control of herself and was still suffering from severe shock. One can't be courageous non-stop, twenty-four hours a day. This was the only possible explanation.

*

'Chief, Cicco De Cicco says he's gonna get on it straight-away and so the pitchers'll be ready round nine aclack t'morrow morning.'

'I want you to pick them up yourself.'

Catarella suddenly assumed a mysterious manner, leaned forward, and said in a low voice:

'Are wese the only twos that knows about this, Chief?'

Montalbano nodded, and Catarella walked out of the office stiff-legged, knees straight, arms swinging out from his sides with fingers spread. The pride of sharing a secret with his boss had changed him from a dog into a strutting peacock.

*

The inspector got in his car to go home, lost in thought. But could that confused tangle of meaningless words and indefinable images that passed now and then through his head be really called thought? His mind seemed to have gone awry like a television set when the picture breaks apart into a sort of grainy zigzag of muddled interference that prevents you from watching what you want to watch and at the same time gives you a faded image of another simultaneous programme, and you're forced to fiddle with the settings, trying to find the cause of the disturbance and to make it go away.

Suddenly Montalbano no longer knew where he was. He no longer recognized the habitual landscape along the road to Marinella. The houses were different, the shops were different, the people were different. Jesus, where had he ended up? He must certainly have made a wrong turn. But how was that possible, since he'd been taking this road at least twice a day for years?

He pulled over, stopped, had a look around, and then understood. Without realizing or wanting to, he'd taken the road to the Mistrettas' villa. For a brief moment, his hands on the steering wheel and his feet on the pedals had acted on their own, without his taking the slightest notice. This happened to him sometimes. That is, his body would do things quite independently, as though not connected to his brain. And when it did this, there was no point in opposing it, because there always turned out to be a reason.

What to do now? Turn around or continue? Naturally, he continued.

When he entered the living room, there were seven

people there listening to Minutolo. They were standing around a big table that had been moved from its corner to the middle of the room. Spread out on the table was a giant map of Vigàta and surroundings, a military sort of map that showed everything down to the street lamps and back alleys where only dogs and goats went to pee.

From his headquarters, Commander-in-Chief Minutolo ordered his men to conduct more intensive, and hopefully fruitful, searches. Fazio was in his usual place. By this point he had merged with the armchair in front of the little table holding the telephone and its related contraptions. Minutolo looked surprised to see Montalbano. Fazio made as if to get up.

'What is it? Did something happen?' asked Minutolo.

'No, no, it's nothing,' said Montalbano, who was just as surprised to find himself there.

Some of those present greeted him, and he replied vaguely.

'I'm giving out orders for—' Minutolo began.

'I can see that,' said Montalbano.

'Did you wish to say something?' Minutolo politely invited him.

'Yes. No shooting. For any reason.'

'May I ask why?'

The question had been asked by a young guy, an up-and-coming assistant inspector, well dressed, quick-tongued, and well toned, with a lock of hair falling rakishly onto his forehead. He looked like a social-climbing business type. One saw so many of his ilk nowadays. A rapidly proliferating race of idiots. Montalbano took an immediate dislike to him.

'Because once, somebody like you shot and killed some wretch who had kidnapped a girl. The search went on, but in vain. The only person who could say where the girl was being held could no longer speak. She was found a month later, bound hand and foot, dead of starvation and dehydration. Satisfied?'

A heavy silence descended. Why the hell had he come back to the villa? Was he, the old cop, merely turning uselessly round and round like a screw stripped of its threads?

He needed a sip of water. There had to be a kitchen somewhere in there. He found it at the end of a corridor. In the kitchen was a nurse, fiftyish and chubby, with an open, friendly face.

'You're Inspector Montalbano, aren't you? Would you like something?' she asked with a sympathetic smile.

'Yes, a glass of water, please.'

The woman poured him a glass of mineral water from a bottle she'd extracted from the refrigerator. As Montalbano drank, she filled a hot-water bottle with steaming water and made as if to leave.

'Just a minute,' the inspector said. 'Where's Mr Mistretta?'

'He's sleeping. It's what the doctor wanted. And he's

right. I gave him some tranquillizers and sleeping pills, as he told me.'

'And Mrs Mistretta? Is she better? Worse? Any news?'

'The only news we'll ever hear of that poor woman is when she dies.'

'Is she in her right mind?'

'Sometimes yes, sometimes no. But even when she seems to understand, in my opinion she doesn't.'

'Could I see her?'

'Follow me.'

Montalbano felt apprehensive. But he knew well that it was a false apprehension, dictated by his desire to postpone an encounter that would be very hard for him to bear.

'What if she asks who I am?'

'Are you kidding? That would be a miracle.'

Halfway down the corridor there was a broad, comfortable staircase leading upstairs, where there was another corridor, this one with six doors.

'That's Mr Mistretta's bedroom; that's the bathroom, and that's the lady's bedroom. It's easier for the help if she sleeps alone. Those doors across the hall are the girl's room – poor thing! – another bathroom, and a guest room,' the nurse explained.

'Could I see Susanna's room?'

'Certainly.'

He opened the door, poked his head in, and turned

on the light. A small bed, armoire, two chairs, a small table with books, a bookcase. All in perfect order. And almost totally anonymous, like a hotel room only temporarily inhabited. Nothing personal, no posters, no photographs. Like the cell of a lay nun. He turned off the light and closed the door. The nurse gently opened the other door. At the same moment, the inspector's forehead and palms broke into a heavy sweat. An uncontrollable terror always came over him whenever he found himself face to face with a dying person. He didn't know what to do. He had to give strict orders to his legs to prevent them from running away of their own accord and dragging him along with them. A dead body didn't frighten him. It was the imminence of death that shook him to the depths of his soul.

He managed to get hold of himself and cross the threshold. Then began his personal descent into hell. He was immediately assailed by the same unbearable odour he had smelled in the room of the legless man, the husband of the woman who sold eggs. Except that here the odour was denser. It stuck to one's skin like a very fine film. It was, moreover, brownish-yellow in colour, with streaks of fiery red. A colour in motion. This had never happened before. The colours evoked by smells had always seemed as though painted on canvas. They held still. Now, however, the red streaks were starting to form a whirlpool. By this point the sweat had drenched his shirt. The woman's regular bed had been replaced by a hospital bed whose whiteness sliced through Montalbano's memory and tried to pull him backwards, to the days of his recovery. Beside the bed were oxygen canisters, an IV stand, and some complicated paraphernalia on a small table. A small cart (also white, for Christ's sake!) was literally covered with vials, small bottles, gauze, measuring glasses, and other containers of varying size. From where he had stopped, barely two steps inside the door, the bed looked empty to him. No human contour could be seen under the taut covers. Even the two pointed mounds formed by the feet when one lies supine were missing. And that sort of strange grey ball forgotten on the pillow was too small to be a head; perhaps it was a large rubber enema syringe whose colour had faded. He advanced another two steps and froze in horror. That thing on the pillow was indeed a human head that had nothing human about it, a hairless, dried-up tangle of wrinkles so deep they looked like they'd been carved with a drill bit. Its mouth was open, a black hole without so much as a hint of white teeth. He had once seen something similar in a magazine, the handiwork of headhunters, practised on their prey. As he stood there staring, unable to move and almost not believing his eyes, out of the hole that was the mouth came a sound created only by the dry, burnt-up throat:

'Ghanna . . .'

'She's calling her daughter,' said the nurse.

Montalbano backpedalled, stiff-legged, knees refusing to bend. To avoid falling, he leaned on a side table.

Then the unexpected happened. *Clack.* The jamming of the mechanism in his head rang out like a pistol shot. Why? It certainly wasn't three twenty-seven and forty seconds in the morning. He was sure of that. And so? Panic assailed him with the viciousness of a rabid dog. The desperate red of the smell became a vortex that threatened to suck him in. His chin began to tremble. His knees, no longer stiff, turned to jelly. To avoid falling, he clutched the marble top of the side table. Luckily the nurse, who was busy with the dying woman, noticed nothing. Then the part of his brain not yet seized by blind fear reacted, enabling him to respond properly. That Thing which had marked him as the bullet penetrated his flesh was trying to tell him that it was here, too, in this very room. Lurking in a corner, ready to appear at the right moment and in the form most appropriate — bullet, tumour, flesh-burning fire, life-drowning water. It was merely a presence made manifest. It didn't concern him. It wasn't his turn yet. And this sufficed to give him some strength. At that moment he noticed a photograph in a silver frame on the side table. A man, Mr Mistretta, was holding the hand of a girl of about ten, Susanna, who in turn held the hand of an attractive, healthy, smiling woman full of life, Signora Giulia. The inspector kept staring at that happy face, to cancel out the image of the other face on the pillow, if one could still call it that. Then he turned on his heel and went out, forgetting to say goodbye to the nurse.

*

He raced like a madman toward Marinella, got home, pulled up, got out of the car but did not go inside. Instead he ran down the beach to the water, took off his clothes, waited a few seconds for the cold night air to chill his skin, then began to advance slowly into the water. With each step the cold cut him with a thousand blades, but he needed to clean his skin, flesh, bones, and still further within, down to his very soul.

He started to swim. But after about ten strokes, a hand armed with a dagger must have emerged from the black waters and stabbed him in the same spot as his wound. At least that was how it seemed to him, so sudden and violent was the pain. It began at the wound and spread throughout his body, becoming unbearable, paralysing. His left arm froze up, and it was all he could do to turn over on his back and do the dead man's float.

Or was he dying in earnest? No, by this point he darkly knew that it was not his fate to die in the water.

Finally, and ever so slowly, he was able to move again.

*

He swam back to shore, picked up his clothes, and smelled his arm, seeming still to detect a trace of the horrendous stench of the dying woman's chamber. The salt water hadn't succeeded in getting rid of it. He would have to wash every pore in his skin, one by one. Panting as he climbed the steps of the veranda, he tapped at the French doors.

'Who is it?' Livia asked from within.

'Open up, I'm freezing.'

Livia opened the door and saw him standing there naked, dripping wet and purple with cold. She started crying.

'Livia, please . . .'

'You're insane, Salvo! You want to die! And you want to kill me, too! What did you do? Why? Why?'

Despairing, she followed him into the bathroom. The inspector covered his entire body with liquid soap, and when he was all yellow he stepped into the shower stall, turned on the water, and began scraping his skin with a piece of pumice stone. Livia, who'd stopped crying, looked at him petrified. He let the water run a long time, nearly emptying the tank on the roof.

As soon as he got out of the shower, Montalbano asked wild-eyed:

'Can you smell me?'

And as he was asking this question, he took a whiff of his arm. He looked like a hunting dog.

'But what's got into you?' Livia asked, distressed.

'Just come here and smell me, please.'

Livia obeyed, running her nose over Salvo's chest.

'What do you smell?'

'Your skin.'

'Are you sure?'

Finally satisfied, the inspector put on a clean set of underwear, a shirt, and a pair of jeans.

They went into the living room. Montalbano sat down in an armchair, Livia settled into the one beside it. For a short spell neither said a word. Then, with her voice still unsteady, Livia asked:

'Better now?'

'Better.'

Another stretch of silence. Then Livia again:

'Are you hungry?'

'I'm hoping I will be soon.'

More silence. Then Livia ventured:

'Want to tell me about it?'

'It's hard.'

'Just try, please.'

And so he told her about it. It took time, for it really was hard for him to find the right words to describe what he had seen. And what he had felt.

When he had finished, Livia asked a question, only one, but it hit the nail on the head.

'Would you explain to me why you went to see her? What need was there?'

Need. Was that the right word? Or the wrong word? True, there was no need, but at the same time, inexplicably, there was.

Ask my hands and feet, he would have liked to reply. Better not delve too deeply. There was still too much confusion in his head. He threw up his hands.

'I can't explain it, Livia.'

As he was saying these words, he realized they were only half true.

They talked a while more, but Montalbano's appetite did not return. His stomach was still in knots.

'Do you think Peruzzo will pay?' Livia asked as they were about to get into bed.

It was the question of the day. Inevitable.

'He'll pay, he'll pay.'

He's already paying, he wanted to add, but said nothing.

*

As he held her tight and kissed her upon entering her, Livia sensed that he was sending a desperate plea for consolation.

'Can't you feel that I'm here?' she whispered in his ear.

TWELVE

When he awoke, it was already broad daylight. Maybe there had been no *clack* that night, or if there had, it hadn't been loud enough to make him open his eyes. It was time to get up, but he chose to lie in bed instead. Though he said nothing to Livia, his bones ached, clearly a consequence of his swim the evening before. And the fresh scar on his shoulder had turned purple and throbbed. Livia noticed that something wasn't right, but decided not to ask any questions.

*

Between one thing and another, he arrived at the office a little late.

'Ahh, Chief, Chief! The pitchers Cicco De Cicco made for you's blown up on your desk!' Catarella said, looking around with suspicion, as soon as the inspector walked in.

De Cicco had, in fact, done an excellent job. In the

enlargements it became clear that the crack in the concrete just under the rim of the basin wasn't a crack at all. It was a deceptive play of light and shadow created by a piece of string hanging from a nail. Attached to the other end of the string was a large thermometer of the sort used to measure the temperature of must. Both the string and thermometer were black from prior use and the soot that had accumulated on them.

There was no doubt in Montalbano's mind: the kidnappers had stuck the girl in a long-abandoned wine vat. So there had to be a press nearby, at a higher level. But why hadn't they bothered to remove the thermometer? Perhaps they hadn't paid any heed to it, having got used to seeing the vat the way it had always been. If you see something enough times you often end up not noticing it any more. Whatever the case, this discovery greatly reduced the area of the search. They were no longer looking for a secluded country cottage, but a veritable farmstead, one perhaps partially in ruin.

He immediately got on the phone to Minutolo and told him of his discovery. Minutolo thought this was a very important development and said that since this considerably lessened the number of targets for their search, he would immediately issue new orders to the men out scouring the countryside.

Then he asked:

'What do you think of the news?'

'What news?'

'Didn't you see TeleVigàta's eight o'clock report?'

'Do you think the first thing I do in the morning is turn on the TV?'

'The kidnappers phoned TeleVigàta, and the TV station recorded everything, then played the recording on the air. The same disguised voice. He says that "the person concerned" has until tomorrow evening. Otherwise nobody will ever see Susanna again.'

Montalbano felt a cold shudder run up his back.

'They've invented the multimedia kidnapping. Didn't they say anything else?'

'I've reported the whole call to you word for word. In fact, they're sending me the tape in a little bit, if you want to come and hear it. The judge is up in arms, he wants to put Ragonese in jail. And you know something? I'm starting to get seriously worried.'

'Me too,' said Montalbano.

So the kidnappers no longer deigned to call the Mistretta home. They had achieved their goal, which was to involve Antonio Peruzzo without ever mentioning his name. Public opinion was unanimously against him. Montalbano was now certain that if the kidnappers ended up killing Susanna, people would hold it not against them but against the uncle, who had refused to do his duty and intervene. Kill? Wait a second. The kidnappers never used that word. They clearly spoke good Italian and knew what to do with the language. They'd said that nobody would ever see the girl again. And when speaking to common folk, a word like *kill* would certainly have made more of an impression. So why hadn't they used it? He seized upon this linguistic fact with all the intensity of his despair. It was like holding onto a blade of grass to keep from falling off a cliff. Perhaps the kidnappers intended to leave a margin for negotiation and did so by avoiding the use of a verb from which there was no return. Whatever the case, one had to act fast. But how?

*

That afternoon Mimì Augello, who'd got sick of lolling about the house, popped up at the office with two bits of news.

The first was that late that morning, Signora Valeria, Antonio Peruzzo's wife, when about to get in her car in a Montelusa car park, was recognized by three women, who surrounded her, shoved her, knocked her to the ground, and started spitting at her, screaming that she ought to be ashamed of herself and should advise her husband to stop wasting time and pay the ransom. More people, meanwhile, had gathered round to lend support to the three women. What saved Signora Valeria was a patrol of Carabinieri that happened to be passing by. At the hospital, the engineer's wife was found to have contusions, bruises, and cuts.

The second bit of news was that two large trucks belonging to Peruzzo Ltd had been set on fire. To avoid any misunderstandings or misinterpretations, on a wall nearby someone had written PAY UP NOW, IDIOT!

'If the kidnappers kill Susanna,' Mimì concluded, 'Peruzzo's gonna get lynched.'

'Do you think the whole thing's going to come to a bad end?' asked Montalbano.

'No,' Mimì said at once, without having to think twice.

'But say the engineer doesn't pay a cent? The kidnappers have sent him a kind of ultimatum.'

'Ultimatums are made to be violated. They'll come to an agreement, you'll see.'

'How's Beba doing?' asked the inspector, changing the subject.

'Pretty well, actually. By the way, Livia came by to see us, and Beba told her we were planning to ask you to be our son's godfather at the baptism.'

No, come on! Was the whole town set on making him godfather?

'And that's the way you inform me?'

'Why, you want a notarized document or something? Did you somehow imagine we wouldn't ask you?'

'Of course not, but—'

'Anyway, Salvo, I know you too well. If I hadn't asked you, you would have felt offended and pulled a long face on me.'

Montalbano realized it was best to steer the conversation away from his character, which lent itself to contradictory interpretations.

'And what did Livia say?'

'She said you would be overjoyed, especially since it would even things out, though I don't know what she meant by that.'

'Me neither,' Montalbano lied.

Of course he knew exactly what she'd meant: a criminal's son and a policeman's son, both with him as their godfather. That would even things out, according to Livia, who, when she put her mind to it, could be just as mean as him, if not more.

＊

It was now evening. He was about to leave the station to go home when Nicolò Zito called.

'I haven't got any time to explain 'cause I'm about to go on the air,' he said in a rush. 'Watch my newscast.'

The inspector dashed down to the cafe. There were about thirty people there, and the television was tuned to the Free Channel. A message on the screen read: IN A FEW MINUTES, AN IMPORTANT ANNOUNCEMENT ON THE MISTRETTA KIDNAPPING. He ordered a beer. The message disappeared, giving way to the news logo. Then Nicolò appeared, sitting behind his customary glass desk. He was wearing the face he reserved for momentous occasions.

'This afternoon,' he said, 'we were contacted by Francesco Luna, a lawyer who has defended the concerns of Engineer Antonio Peruzzo more than once. He asked us to allow him the airtime to make an announcement. It is not an interview. He also stipulated we must not follow his declaration with any commentary of our own. We decided to accept his conditions, despite their restrictions, because this is a very important moment for the fate of Susanna Mistretta, and Mr Luna's words may go a long way towards clarifying matters and leading to a happy resolution of this delicate and dramatic case.'

Cut. A typical lawyer's office appeared. Dark wood bookcases full of unread books, collections of laws dating back to the late nineteenth century but surely still in effect, because in Italy no part of any hundred-year-old law is ever thrown away. Same as with pigs. Mr Luna looked exactly the way his name would suggest: lunar. Round, full-moon face, obese, full-moon body. Obviously influenced by this fact, the lighting engineer bathed the whole scene in a blue, lunar light. The lawyer was spilling out of an armchair. In his hand he held a sheet of paper, which he looked down at from time to time as he spoke.

'I speak on behalf of my client, Engineer Antonio Peruzzo, who finds himself forced to emerge from his dutiful silence to stem the rising tide of lies and iniquities that have been unleashed against him. Mr Peruzzo wants everyone to know that, being well aware of the difficult economic conditions of the Mistretta family, he put himself at the full disposal of Susanna Mistretta's abductors the day after her kidnapping. Unfortunately, however, and inexplicably, Mr Peruzzo's readiness to cooperate has not been returned in kind by the kidnappers. This being the case, Mr Peruzzo can only reaffirm the commitment he has already made, not only with the abductors, but with his own conscience.'

Everyone gathered at the bar burst out laughing, drowning out the statement that followed.

'If the engineer's made a commitment with his conscience, the girl's had it!' one of them shouted, saying what everyone was thinking.

Things were so bad that if Peruzzo himself went on TV to announce to everyone that he had decided to pay the ransom, everyone would think he was paying with counterfeit bills.

The inspector went back to the office and rang Minutolo.

'The judge just called and said he'd also seen the lawyer's statement. He wants me to go and see Luna and get some clarifications. What you might call an informal visit. And respectful. In short, we need to put on kid gloves. I've already phoned Luna, who knows me. He said he's available. Does he know you?'

'Dunno. He knows who I am.'

'You want to come, too?'

'Sure. Give me the address.'

*

Minutolo was waiting for him at the front door. He'd come in his own car, like Montalbano. A wise precaution, since many of Luna's clients would probably have a heart attack if they saw a police car parked in front of their lawyer's place. The house was heavily and luxuriously furnished. A housekeeper dressed like a housekeeper showed them into the same study they'd seen on tele-vision. She gestured for them to make themselves comfortable.

'Mr Luna will be right with you.'

Minutolo and Montalbano sat down in two armchairs in a sort of sitting room that had been set up in a corner. They nearly disappeared inside their respective, enormous easy chairs, custom-made for elephants and Mr Luna. The wall behind the desk was entirely covered by photographs of varying size, all duly framed. There must have been at least fifty. They looked like ex-votos hung to commem-orate and thank some miracle-working saint. The lighting in the room made it impossible to tell who the people in the photos were. Maybe they were clients saved from the nation's prisons by that blend of oratory, cunning, corrup-tion, and survival instinct that was Mr Luna. Given, however, that the host was late in arriving, the inspector couldn't resist, and he got up and went over to look at the photos. They were all of politicians: senators, deputies of the chamber, ministers, former or current undersec-retaries. All signed and dedicated to the 'dear' or 'dearest'

Mr Luna. Montalbano sat back down. He now understood why the commissioner had advised them to proceed
with caution.

'My dear friends!' said the lawyer upon entering the
room. 'Please don't get up! Can I get you anything? I have
whatever you want.'

'No, thank you,' said Minutolo.

'Yes, please, I'd like a daiquiri,' said Montalbano.

The lawyer gave him a befuddled look.

'Actually, I don't—'

'Never mind,' the inspector conceded, gesturing as if
brushing away a fly.

As the lawyer was easing himself onto the sofa,
Minutolo shot a dirty look at Montalbano, as if to tell
him to stop clowning around.

'So, shall I speak first, or do you want to ask
questions?'

'You speak first,' said Minutolo.

'All right if I take notes?' asked Montalbano, sticking
his hand in his jacket pocket, which contained nothing
whatsoever.

'No! Why do you need to do that?' Luna burst out.

Minutolo's eyes implored Montalbano to stop making
trouble.

'OK, OK,' said the inspector, conciliatory.

'Where were we?' asked the lawyer, confused.

'We hadn't started yet,' said Montalbano.

Luna surely noticed the mockery, but pretended not

to. Montalbano understood that the lawyer understood, and so decided to knock it off.

'Oh, yes. Well, around ten a.m. on the day after the abduction, my client received an anonymous phone call.'

'When?!' Minutolo and Montalbano asked in unison.

'Around ten a.m. on the day after the abduction.'

'You mean barely fourteen hours after?' asked Minutolo, still bewildered.

'Exactly,' the lawyer continued. 'A man's voice informed him that, since the abductors were aware that the Mistrettas were not in a position to pay the ransom, for all intents and purposes they considered him the only person who could satisfy their demands. They said they would call back at three in the afternoon. My client . . .' (Every time he said 'my client' he made the kind of face a nurse might make when wiping the sweat off her moribund patient's forehead.) '. . . rushed here to see me. We quickly came to the conclusion that my client had been skilfully cornered. And that the kidnappers were holding all the cards. If they wanted to drag him into this, there wasn't much we could do about it. Shirking his responsibility to the girl would gravely damage his reputation, which had already been harmed by a few unpleasant episodes. And it might irreparably compromise his political ambitions. Which I think has already happened, unfortunately. He was supposed to be on the ticket in the next elections, in a district where he would have been a certainty.'

'No point in asking with what party,' said Montalbano, looking up at a photo of Berlusconi in a jogging outfit.

'Yes, no point indeed,' the lawyer said sternly, then continued, 'I gave him some suggestions. The kidnappers called back at three. When asked, at my suggestion, for proof that the girl was alive, they replied that this would soon be broadcast on TeleVigàta. Which in fact is exactly what happened. They asked for six billion lire. They wanted my client to buy a new mobile phone and go immediately to Palermo, without telling anyone, except his bankers. One hour later they called back for the mobile phone number. My client had no choice but to obey, and withdrew the six billion in record time. On the evening of the following day, they called again, and he told them he was ready to pay. But since then, inexplicably, he has received no further instruction, as I said on TV.'

'Why didn't Peruzzo authorize you to make that statement any earlier than this evening?'

'Because the kidnappers had warned him against any such action. He was not to grant any interviews or make any statement at all, but to disappear for a few days.'

'And did they withdraw the warning?'

'No. My client decided to take the initiative himself, which is extremely risky ... But he can't stand it any longer ... especially after that cowardly attack on his wife, and after his trucks were burned.'

'Do you know where Peruzzo is now?'

'No.'

'Do you know his mobile phone number – the new one?'

'No.'

'How do you stay in touch?'

'He calls me. From a public phone.'

'Does he have email?'

'Yes, but he left his computer at home. That's what they told him to do, and he has obeyed.'

'In short, are you telling us that any freeze of his assets would be useless at this point, since Peruzzo's already got the ransom money on him?'

'Exactly.'

'Do you think he'll phone you the moment he knows where and when he's supposed to deliver the ransom?'

'What for?'

'Are you aware that if he did, you would be legally obligated to inform us at once?'

'Of course I am. And I'm ready to do as required. Except that my client won't be calling me, or at least not until it's all been taken care of.'

Minutolo had asked all the questions. This time Montalbano decided to speak.

'What size?'

'I don't understand,' said the lawyer.

'What size notes did they want?'

'Ah, yes. Five-hundred euros.'

Strange. Big notes. Easier to carry around, but much harder to spend.

'Do you know if your client...' (the lawyer made the nurse-face) '...managed to write down the serial numbers?'

'I don't know.'

The lawyer looked at his gold Rolex and grimaced.

'And there you have it,' he said, standing up.

*

They stopped to chat a moment outside the lawyer's house.

'Poor Peruzzo,' the inspector said by way of comment. 'He tried to cover himself immediately. He'd pinned his hopes on a quick kidnapping, so people wouldn't find out, whereas—'

'That's one thing that has me worried,' said Minutolo. And he began to clarify: 'From what the lawyer said, if the kidnappers immediately contacted Peruzzo—'

'Almost twelve hours before they made their first phone contact with us,' Montalbano cut in, 'then they played us like puppets at the puppet theatre. Because those guys were play-acting with us. They knew from the very first moment who they wanted to force to pay the ransom. They've made the two of us waste a lot of time, and they've made Fazio lose sleep. They're smart. In the final analysis, the messages they sent to the Mistretta home were scenes from an old script, more than anything else. They showed us what we wanted to see, told us what we expected to hear.'

'Based on what the lawyer said,' Minutolo resumed, 'the kidnappers theoretically had the situation under control less than twenty-four hours after the abduction. One call to Peruzzo, and he would hand over the money. Except that they never got back to him. Why? Had they run into trouble? Maybe the men we have out scouring the countryside are hampering their freedom of movement? Maybe we should let up a little?'

'What are you afraid of, exactly?'

'That if those guys feel threatened, they'll do something stupid.'

'You're forgetting one basic thing.'

'What?'

'That the kidnappers have remained in contact with the television stations.'

'So why won't they get in touch with Peruzzo?'

'Because they want him to stew in his own juices first,' said the inspector.

'But the more time passes, the greater their risk!'

'They're well aware of that. And I think they also know they've played out the string as far as it'll go. I'm convinced it's only a matter of hours before Susanna goes home.'

Minutolo looked befuddled.

'What! This morning you didn't seem at all—'

'This morning the lawyer hadn't yet spoken on television and hadn't yet used an adverb he repeated when speaking to us. He was shrewd. He indirectly told the kidnappers to stop playing games.'

'Excuse me,' said Minutolo, completely confused, 'but what adverb did he use?'

'Inexplicably.'

'And what does it mean?'

'It means that he, the lawyer, knew the explanation perfectly well.'

'I haven't understood a damned thing.'

'Forget it. What are you going to do now?'

'Report to the judge.'

THIRTEEN

Livia wasn't at home. The table was set for two people, and beside her plate was a note.

I've gone to the movies with my friend.
Wait for me to eat dinner.

He went and had a shower, then sat down in front of the television. The Free Channel was showing a debate on Susanna's abduction, with Nicolò as moderator. Taking part in the discussion were a monsignor, three lawyers, a retired judge, and a journalist. Half an hour into the programme, the debate openly turned into a kind of trial of Antonio Peruzzo. Or, more than a trial, an out-and-out lynching. When all was said and done, nobody believed what Luna the lawyer had said. None of those present seemed convinced by the story that Peruzzo had the money ready and was only waiting to hear from the suddenly silent kidnappers. Logically speaking, it was in their interest to get their hands on the money as quickly as possible, free the girl, and disappear. The more time they wasted, the greater the risk. And so? It seemed natural to think that the person responsible for the delay in Susanna's liberation was none other than Peruzzo himself, who – as the monsignor insinuated – was dragging things out trying to extract some miserable little discount on the ransom. The way he was acting, would he get any discount when he appeared before God on Judgement Day? In conclusion, it seemed clear that, once the girl was freed, a change of scene was Peruzzo's only option.

Talk about political ambitions gone up in smoke! He wasn't even welcome any more in Montelusa, Vigàta, or environs.

✳

This time the *clack* at three twenty-seven and forty seconds woke him up. He realized his brain was clear and functioning perfectly, and took advantage of this to review the entire kidnapping case, starting from Catarella's first phone call. He stopped thinking around five thirty, when he suddenly began to feel sleepy. As he was sinking into unconsciousness, the telephone rang and, luckily, Livia didn't hear it. The clock said five forty-seven. It was Fazio, who was very excited.

'Susanna's been freed.'
'Oh, really? How is she?'
'Fine.'

'See you later,' Montalbano concluded.

And he went back to bed.

He told Livia the news the moment she began to move in bed, showing the first signs of waking up. She leapt out of bed and onto her feet, as if she'd seen a spider between the sheets.

'When did you find out?'

'Fazio called. It was around six.'

'Why didn't you tell me immediately?'

'Was I supposed to wake you up?'

'Yes. You know how anxiously I've been following this whole ordeal. You let me keep sleeping on purpose!'

'If that's the way you want to see it, fine, I admit my guilt, end of subject. Now calm down.'

But Livia felt like making trouble. She eyed him with disdain.

'And I don't understand how you can lie there in bed, instead of going to see Minutolo to get more information, to find out—'

'To find out what? If you want more information, turn on the TV.'

'Sometimes your indifference drives me crazy!'

She went and turned on the television. Montalbano, for his part, locked himself in the bathroom and took his time. Obviously to get on his nerves, Livia kept the volume high. As he was drinking his coffee in the kitchen, he could hear angry voices, sirens, screeching tyres. He could barely hear the telephone when it rang. He went into the dining room. Everything was vibrating from the infernal noise emanating from the set.

'Livia, would you please turn that down?'

Muttering to herself, Livia obeyed. The inspector picked up the receiver.

'Montalbano? What's wrong, aren't you coming?'

It was Minutolo.

'What for?'

Minutolo seemed stunned.

'Er ... I dunno ... I thought you'd be pleased ...'

'Anyway, I have the impression you're under siege.'

'That's true. There are dozens of journalists, photographers, and cameramen outside the gate ... I had to call in reinforcements. The judge and the commissioner should be here soon. It's a mess.'

'How's Susanna doing?'

'A bit the worse for wear, but basically all right. Her uncle examined her and found her in good physical condition.'

'How was she treated?'

'She said they never once made a violent gesture. On the contrary.'

'How many were there?'

'She saw only two hooded men. Obviously peasants.'

'How did they release her?'

'She said that last night, when she was sleeping, they woke her up, made her put on a hood, tied her hands behind her back, took her out of the vat, and made her get in the boot of a car. They drove for over two hours, she said. Then the car stopped. They made her get out, had her walk for half an hour, then loosened the knots around her wrists and made her sit down. Then they left.'

'And they never spoke to her at any point during all this?'

'Never. It took her a while to free her hands and remove the hood. It was pitch-black outside. She hadn't the slightest idea where she was, but she didn't lose heart. She managed to get her bearings and headed in the direction of Vigàta. At some point she realized she was near La Cucca, you know, that village—'

'Yeah, I know. Go on.'

'It's a little over two miles from her villa. She walked the distance, arrived at the gate, rang the bell, and Fazio went and let her in.'

'All according to script, in other words.'

'What do you mean?'

'I mean they keep enacting the same drama that we've become accustomed to seeing. A sham performance. The real show they put on for one spectator alone, Antonio Peruzzo, and they asked him to join in. Then there was a third show aimed at the general public. How was Peruzzo? Did he play his part well?'

'Frankly, Montalbano, I don't understand what you're saying.'

'Have you succeeded in getting in touch with Peruzzo?'

'Not yet.'

'So what happens next?'

'The judge is going to hear Susanna's story, then this afternoon there'll be a press conference. Aren't you going to come?'

'Not even if you put a gun to my head.'

*

He was barely in the doorway to his office when the phone rang.

'Chief? There's some jinnelman onna line says he's the moon. So, tinkin he's makin some kinda joke, I says I'm the sun. He got pissed off. I tink he's insane.'

'Put him on.'

What did the devoted nurse want from him?

'Inspector Montalbano? Good morning. This is Francesco Luna, the lawyer.'

'Good morning, sir. What can I do for you?'

'First of all, my compliments on your receptionist.'

'Well, sir, you see—'

'*Pay them no mind, but look and move on,* as the poet says. Let's drop it. I'm calling you only to remind you that your pointless, offensive sarcasm yesterday, toward myself and my client, was inexcusable. You know, I have the misfortune, or good luck, of having an elephant's memory.'

Because you, sir, ARE an elephant, the inspector wanted to say, but he managed to restrain himself.

'Please explain what you mean, sir.'

'Yesterday evening, when you and your colleague came to my house, you were convinced my client would not pay the ransom, whereas, as you have seen—'

'Excuse me, but you're mistaken. I was convinced that your client, like it or not, *would* pay the ransom. Have you managed to get in touch with him?'

'He phoned me last night, after doing what he needed to do. What people expected of him.'

'Can we talk to him?'

'He doesn't feel up to it yet. He's just been through a terrible ordeal.'

'You mean the ordeal of three million euros in bills of five hundred?'

'Yes. Three million, stuffed in a suitcase or a duffel bag, I'm not sure which.'

'Do you know where they told him to drop the money off?'

'Well, they phoned him yesterday evening around nine and described in minute detail a road he was supposed to take to a small overpass, the only one there is along the road to Brancato. With hardly any traffic. Under the overpass, he would find a sort of little well covered by a lid that could be easily lifted. All he needed to do was put the suitcase or duffel inside, close it back up, and leave. My client arrived on the spot shortly before midnight. He did exactly as he was ordered to do, then quickly went away.'

'Thank you, Mr Luna.'

'Excuse me, Inspector. I want to ask a favour of you.'

'What kind of favour?'

'I would like you to help us resuscitate my client's reputation, which has been so gravely compromised. And this you can do by honestly saying exactly what you know. Not one word more, not one word less.'

'May I ask who the other resuscitators are?'

'Myself, Inspector Minutolo, all the engineer's friends from within and without the party – in short, everyone who's had a chance to know—'

'If the opportunity presents itself, I'll be sure to do so.'

'I appreciate it.'

The telephone rang again.

'Chief, iss Dr Latte with an *S* at the end.'

That is, Dr Lattes, chief of the commissioner's cabinet, a churchgoing, cloying sort of man, subscriber to the *L'Osservatore Romano,* and known informally as Caffè-Lattes.

'My dear Inspector! How are you doing?'

'I can't complain.'

'Let us thank the Blessed Virgin! And how's the family?'

What a pain in the arse! He had got it in his head that the inspector had a family, and there was no way to shake him out of this conviction. If he ever found out that Montalbano was a bachelor, the shock might be lethal.

'Fine, thanking the Blessed Virgin.'

'Well, on behalf of Commissioner Bonetti-Alderighi, I'm inviting you to attend the press conference that will be held at Montelusa Central Police at five thirty this evening, concerning the felicitous outcome of the Mistretta kidnapping. The commissioner would like to make it clear, however, that only your attendance is being requested – that is, you will not be asked to speak.'

'Thank the Blessed Virgin,' Montalbano muttered under his breath.

'What was that? I didn't hear.'

'I said I was wondering something. As you know, I'm still convalescing, and was called back into service only because—'

'I know, I know. And so?'

'So could I be exempted from attending the press conference? I'm a bit tired out.'

Lattes couldn't hide how happy the inspector's request made him. Montalbano was always considered a loose cannon at these official functions.

'But of course! Of course! Take good care of yourself, dear friend. But consider yourself on duty until further notice.'

*

Surely someone had already thought of writing *The Perfect Investigator's Handbook*. It had to exist, since there was, after all, a *Junior Woodchucks' Guidebook*. And it was certainly written by Americans, who were capable of publishing handbooks on how to put buttons in buttonholes. Montalbano, however, had never seen such a handbook. Nevertheless, somewhere in such a book the writer must surely recommend that the sooner the investigator inspects a crime scene, the better. That is, before the elements — rain, wind, sun, man, animals — so alter the scene that the telltale signs, already barely perceptible, become indecipherable.

Based on what Mr Luna had told him, Montalbano — alone among the investigators — knew where Peruzzo had left the ransom money. It was his duty, he reasoned, to inform Minutolo of this fact at once. Surely the kidnappers had spent a long time hiding in the area around the overpass on the road to Brancato, first making sure there were no policemen lying in ambush, then waiting for Peruzzo's car to arrive, and finally letting a bit more time pass to ensure that all was calm before coming out in the open and picking up the suitcase. And surely they had left some trace of their presence. It was therefore imperative to examine the site before the crime scene was altered (as per aforementioned *Handbook*).

Wait a second, he said to himself as his hand was picking up the telephone. What if Minutolo couldn't go there immediately? Wasn't it better to get in his car and have a first look himself? Just an initial, superficial inspection? If, then, he discovered anything important, he would alert Minutolo so a more thorough examination could be conducted.

Such was how he tried to quiet his conscience, which had been muttering to itself for some time. His conscience, however, was stubborn. Not only would it not be silenced, but it made its own feelings known.

No point in making excuses, Montalbà. You just want to screw Minutolo, now that the girl's no longer in danger.

'Catarella!'

'Your orders, Chief!'

'Do you know the quickest way to Brancato?'

'Which Brancato, Chief? Upper Brancato or Lower Brancato?'

'Is it so big?'

'Nossir. There's just five hunnert nabitants till yesterday. Fact is, tho, that seeing as how Upper Brancato's been falling down the mountainside below—'

'What do you mean? Are there landslides?'

'Yessir, so, seeing as how there's what you just said there is, they hadda build a new town unner the mountin. But there's fifty old folks din't wanna leave their homes and so now the nabitants been nabitting all apart from nother wuther, wit four hunnert forty-nine b'low 'n' fifty up top.'

'Wait a second. We're missing one inhabitant.'

'Din't I jes say there's five hunnert till yesterday? Yesterday one of 'em died, Chief. My cussin Michele tol' me. He lives out Lower Brancato way.'

Of course! How could Catarella *not* have a relative in that godforsaken village?

'Listen, Cat. If you're driving from Palermo, which comes first, Upper or Lower Brancato?'

'Lower, Chief.'

'And how do you get there?'

The explanation was long and convoluted.

'Listen, Cat. If Inspector Minutolo rings, tell him to call me on the mobile.'

*

He took the *scorrimento veloce*, the 'expressway', for Palermo, which was clogged with traffic. This was a perfectly ordinary two-lane road, slightly broader than normal, but, for no apparent reason, everyone considered it a kind of *autostrada* and therefore drove as though they were on an *autostrada*. Trucks passing trucks, cars racing at ninety miles an hour (since such was the speed limit a cabinet minister, the one ostensibly 'in charge' of such matters, had set for the *autostrade*), tractors, motor scooters, rattle-trap little pickups lost in a tide of mopeds. On both sides, right and left, the road was dotted with little slabs of stone adorned with bouquets of flowers – not for beauty's sake, but to mark the exact spots where dozens of luckless wretches, in cars or on motorbikes, had lost their lives. A continuous commemoration – which nobody, however, gave a damn about.

He turned left at the third intersection. The road was paved but had no markings or signs. He would have to trust in Catarella's directions. By now the landscape had changed. Low, rolling hills, a few vineyards. And not a trace of any villages. He hadn't even crossed another car. He began to get worried. Most importantly, he didn't see another living soul he might ask for directions. All at once he didn't feel like proceeding any farther. But just as he was about to make a U-turn and head back to Vigàta, he saw a cart and horse coming towards him. He decided to ask the driver for help. He drove on a little, and when he was in front of the horse, he stopped, opened the car door, and got out.

'Good day,' he said to the driver.

The driver seemed not to have noticed the inspector. He merely looked straight ahead, reins in hand.

'Likewise,' he replied. Sixtyish and sunburnt, gaunt and dressed in fustian, he was wearing an absurd Borsalino on his head that must have dated back to the fifties.

But he made no motion to stop.

'I wanted to ask you for some information,' said Montalbano, walking beside him.

'Me?' asked the man, half surprised, half worried.

Who else, if not? The horse?

'Yes.'

'Ehhhhh,' said the man, pulling on the reins. The animal stopped.

The man said nothing and kept looking straight ahead. He was waiting to be asked the question.

'Listen, could you tell me how to get to Lower Brancato?'

Reluctantly, as though it cost him great effort, the man on the cart said:

'Keep going straight. Third road on the right. Good day. Ahhh!'

That *ahhh* was directed at the horse, which resumed walking.

*

Half an hour later, Montalbano saw something that looked like a cross between an overpass and a bridge appear in the distance. Unlike a bridge, it had no parapet, but large protective metal screens instead; and unlike an overpass, it was arched like a bridge. In the background loomed a hill on which a group of small, dicelike white houses sat impossibly balanced halfway down the slope. That had to be Upper Brancato, whereas nary a roof of the lower village was visible yet. Whatever the case, he must be close. Montalbano stopped the car about twenty yards from the overpass, got out, and started looking around. The road was distressingly empty. The only other vehicle he'd encountered since the intersection was the cart. He'd also noticed a peasant hoeing. That was all. Once the sun went down and darkness fell, one probably couldn't see anything along that road. There was no sort of lighting whatsoever, no houses that might give off a faint glow at night. So where had the kidnappers taken up position while waiting for Peruzzo's car? And most importantly, how could they have known for certain that the car they saw was indeed Peruzzo's and not another vehicle that by some miracle happened to be passing that way?

Around the overpass — the need for which remained unclear, as well as how or why it had occurred to anyone to build it — there were no bushes or walls to hide behind. Even in the dead of night, the site provided no cover that might prevent one from being seen in the headlights of a passing car. And so?

A dog barked. Spurred by the need to see another living being, Montalbano's eyes scanned the surroundings, searching for it. He found it. It was at the start of the overpass on the right, and he could only see its head. Maybe they'd built it just so dogs and cats could cross the road. Why not, since when it came to public works in Italy, the impossible often became possible? All at once the inspector realized that the kidnappers had hidden in the very spot where the dog was now.

He trudged through the brush, crossed an unmade road, and came to the point where the overpass began. It was hogbacked; that is, sharply curved. Someone who placed himself right at the start of the overpass could not be seen from the road below. He looked carefully down at the ground as the dog backed away, growling, but found nothing of interest, not even a cigarette butt. Then again, why would you find a cigarette butt lying about, now that everyone's been scared to death of smoking by those warnings on packets that say things like 'Smoking gives you cancer'? Even criminals have been giving up the vice, depriving poor policemen of essential clues. Maybe he should write a complaint to the Minister of Health.

He searched the opposite side of the overpass as well. Nothing. He went back to the starting point and lay down on his stomach. He looked down below, pressing his head against the metal screen, and saw, almost vertically beneath him, a stone slab covering the opening to a small well. Seeing Peruzzo's car approach, the kidnappers must certainly have climbed up the overpass and done as he had done — that is, lain down on the ground. And from there, in the glare of the headlamps, they had watched Peruzzo lift the stone lid, place the suitcase in the well, and leave. That must surely be how it went. But he had not accomplished what he had set out to do in coming all the way out here. The kidnappers had left no trace.

He came down from the overpass and went underneath. He studied the slab covering the well. It looked too small for a suitcase to fit inside. He did some quick maths: six billion lire equalled three million one hundred euros, more or less. If each wad contained one hundred notes of five hundred euros, that would make a total of sixty-two wads. Therefore they didn't need a large suitcase. On the contrary. The slab was easy to lift, since it had a sort of iron ring attached to it. He stuck a finger inside the ring and pulled. The slab came off. Montalbano looked inside the well and gasped. There was a duffel bag inside, and it did not look empty. Was Peruzzo's money still in it? Was it possible the kidnappers hadn't picked it up? Then why had they freed the girl?

He knelt, reached down, and grabbed the bag, which was heavy, pulled it out, and set it down on the ground. Taking a deep breath, he opened it. It was filled with wads not of notes, but of old glossy-magazine clippings.

FOURTEEN

The shock sort of pushed him backwards, knocking him down on his bottom. Mouth open in astonishment, he began asking himself some questions. What did this discovery mean? That Engineer Peruzzo himself had filled the bag with scrap paper instead of euros? Was Peruzzo, as far as he knew, a man capable of taking the extreme sort of gamble that would endanger the life of his niece? After thinking about this for a moment, he concluded that the engineer was indeed capable of this and more. In that case, however, the kidnappers' actions became inexplicable. Because there were only two possibilities, there was no getting around it: either the kidnappers had opened the bag on the spot, realized they'd been hoodwinked, and decided nevertheless to release the girl, or else they had fallen into the trap — that is, they'd seen Peruzzo put the bag in the well, had no chance to check it immediately, and, trusting in appearances, had given the order to free Susanna.

Or had Peruzzo somehow known that the kidnappers wouldn't be able to open the bag at once and check its contents, and had gambled against time? Wait. Wrong line of reasoning. No one could have prevented the kidnappers from opening the well whenever they saw fit. Since delivery of the ransom did not necessarily mean the immediate release of the girl, against what 'time' could Peruzzo have gambled? None whatsoever. No matter which way one looked at it, the engineer's trick seemed insane.

As he sat there, stunned, questions riddling his brain like machine-gun fire, he heard a strange sort of ringing and couldn't tell where it was coming from. He decided it must be an approaching flock of sheep. But the sound didn't come any closer, even though it was very close already. Then he realized it must be his mobile phone, which he never used and had only put in his pocket on this occasion.

'Chief, is that you? Fazio here.'

'What is it?'

'Chief, Inspector Minutolo wants me to inform you of something that just happened about forty-five minutes ago. I tried you at the station, at home, and finally Catarella remembered that—'

'OK, fine, tell me what it is.'

'Well, Inspector Minutolo called Luna to find out if he'd heard from Peruzzo. The lawyer said Peruzzo paid the ransom last night and had even explained to him where he'd left the money. And so Inspector Minutolo rushed to the place, which is along the road to Brancato, to conduct a preliminary search. Unfortunately, the newsmen followed right behind him.'

'In short, what did Minutolo want?'

'He says he'd like you to meet him there. I'll tell you what's the quickest way to get—'

But Montalbano had already hung up. Minutolo, his men, and a swarm of journalists, photographers, and cameramen might arrive at any moment. And if they saw him, how would he explain what he was doing there?

Gosh, what a surprise! I was just out tilling the fields . . .

He hastily lowered the duffel bag into the well, closed it with the stone slab, ran to the car, started up the engine, began turning the car around, then stopped. If he went back the same way he'd come, he would surely run into Minutolo and the festive caravan of cars behind him. No, he had best continue on to Lower Brancato.

It took him barely ten minutes to get there. A clean little town, with a tiny piazza, church, town hall, cafe, bank, trattoria, and shoe shop. All around the piazza were granite benches, with some ten men sitting on them, all ageing, old, or decrepit. They weren't talking, weren't moving at all. For a fraction of a second, Montalbano thought they were statues, splendid examples of hyperrealist art. But then one of them, apparently belonging to the decrepit category, suddenly threw his head backwards and laid it against the back of the bench. He was either dead, as seemed quite likely, or had been overcome by a sudden desire to sleep.

The country air had whetted the inspector's appetite. He looked at his watch. Just short of one o'clock. He headed towards the trattoria, then stopped short. What if some journalist got the brilliant idea to make his phone calls from Lower Brancato? No question, of course, that there would be any restaurants in Upper Brancato. But he didn't feel like letting his stomach go empty for too long. The only solution was to run the risk and enter the trattoria in front of him.

Out of the corner of his eye, he saw someone come out from behind the counter and stop to stare at him. The man, fat and forty, approached him with a big smile.

'But ... aren't you Inspector Montalbano?'

'Yes, but ...'

'Iss a real plisure. I'm Michele Zarco.'

He declaimed his first and last names in the tone of someone known to one and all. But since the inspector kept staring at him without a word, he clarified:

'I'm Catarella's cussin.'

*

Michele Zarco, land surveyor and deputy mayor of Brancato, was his salvation. First, he brought him to his house for an informal meal – that is, to eat whatever was available. Nuttin spicial, as he put it. Signora Angila Zarco, a woman of few words, blonde to the point of looking washed out, served them *cavatuna* in tomato sauce that were eminently respectable, followed by *coniglo all'-agrodolce* – sweet-and-sour rabbit – from the day before. Now, preparing *coniglo all'agrodolce* is a complicated matter, because everything depends on the right proportion of vinegar to honey and on making the pieces of rabbit blend properly with the *caponata* in which it must cook. Signora Zarco clearly knew how to go about this, and for good measure had thrown in a sprinkling of toasted ground almonds over the whole thing. On top of this, it is well known that the *coniglo all'agrodolce* you eat the day it is made is one thing, but when eaten the next day it is something else entirely, because it gains considerably in flavour and aroma. In short, Montalbano had a feast.

Then Deputy Mayor Zarco suggested they visit Upper Brancato, just to aid digestion. Naturally they went in Zarco's car. After taking a road that consisted of one sharp turn after another and looked like the X-ray of an intestine, they stopped in the middle of a cluster of houses that would have made an Expressionist set-designer's day. Not a single house stood up straight. They all leaned to the left or the right at angles so extreme that the Tower of Pisa would have looked perfectly perpendicular by comparison. Three or four houses were actually attached to the hillside and jutted out horizontally, as if they had suction cups holding them in place, hidden in the foundations. Two old men walked by talking to each other, but rather loudly, because one was listing sharply to the right, the other to the left. Perhaps they'd been conditioned by the inclinations of the houses in which they lived.

'Shall we go back home for coffee? The missus makes a good cup,' said Zarco, when he saw that Montalbano, under the influence of the surroundings, had started walking askew himself.

When Signora Angila opened the door for them, to Montalbano she looked like a child's drawing: almost albino, her hair braided, her cheeks red. She seemed agitated.

'What's wrong?' her husband asked.

'The TV just said the girl was released but the ransom wasn't paid!'

'Really?!' asked the land surveyor, looking over at Montalbano.

The inspector shrugged and threw his hands up, as if to say he didn't know the first thing about the whole affair.

'Oh, yes,' the woman went on. 'They said the police found Mr Peruzzo's duffel bag, right near here, in fact, and it was filled with newspaper. The newsman wondered how and why the girl was freed. What's clear is that piece-of-slime uncle of hers risked getting her killed!'

No longer Antonio Peruzzo or 'the engineer', but 'that piece of slime', that unnameable shit, that excrescence of sewage. If Peruzzo had indeed wanted to gamble, he'd lost. Although the girl had been freed, he was now forever prisoner of the utter, absolute contempt in which people held him.

✻

The inspector decided not to return to the office but to go back home and watch the press conference in peace. When nearing the overpass, he drove very carefully, in case any stragglers had stayed behind. At any rate, the signs that a horde of policemen, journalists, photographers, and cameramen had passed through were everywhere: empty cans of Coca-Cola, broken beer bottles, crumpled packets of cigarettes. A rubbish dump. They'd even broken the stone slab that covered the little well.

✻

As he was opening the door to his house, he froze. He hadn't called Livia all morning. He'd completely forgotten to tell her he wouldn't make it home for lunch. A squabble was now inevitable, and he had no excuses. The house, however, was empty. Livia had gone out. Entering the bedroom, he saw her open suitcase, half full. He immediately remembered that Livia was supposed to return to Boccadasse the next morning. The holiday time she'd taken to stay beside him at the hospital and during his convalescence was over. He felt a sudden pang in his heart, and a wave of emotion swept over him, treacherous as usual. It was a good thing she wasn't there. He could let himself go without shame. And let himself go he did.

Then he went and washed his face, after which he sat down in the chair in front of the telephone. He opened the phone book. The lawyer had two numbers, one for his home, the other for his office. Montalbano dialled the latter.

'Legal offices of Francesco Luna,' said a female voice.

'This is Inspector Montalbano. Is Mr Luna there?'

'Yes, but he's in a meeting. Let me see if he picks up.'

Various noises, recorded music.

'My dear friend,' said Luna. 'I can't talk to you right now. Are you in your office?'

'No, I'm at home. You want the number?'

'Please.'

Montalbano gave it to him.

'I'll call you back in about ten minutes,' said the lawyer.

*

The inspector noted that during their brief exchange, Luna didn't once call him by his name or title. One could only imagine what sort of clients he was meeting with; no doubt they would have been troubled to hear the word *inspector*.

About half an hour passed, give or take a few minutes, before the phone rang.

'Inspector Montalbano? Please excuse the delay, but first I was with some people and then I thought I'd better call you from a safe phone.'

'What are you saying, Mr Luna? Have the phones to your office been tapped?'

'I'm not sure, but the way things are going ... What did you want to tell me?'

'Nothing you don't already know.'

'Are you referring to the bag full of clippings?'

'Exactly. You realize, of course, that this development is a serious impediment to the resuscitation of Peruzzo's reputation, to which you'd asked me to contribute.'

Silence, as if they'd been cut off.

'Hello?' said Montalbano.

'I'm still here. Answer me sincerely, Inspector: do you think that if I'd known there was only scrap paper inside that well, I would have told you and Inspector Minutolo?'

'No.'

'Well, the moment he heard the news, my client called me up, extremely upset. He was in tears. He realized that this discovery was like cementing his feet and throwing himself into the sea. Death by drowning, with no chance of ever coming back to the surface. Inspector, that duffel bag was not his. He'd put his money in a suitcase.'

'Can he prove it?'

'No.'

'And how does he explain that the police found a duffel instead of a suitcase?'

'He can't explain it.'

'And he'd put the money in this suitcase?'

'Of course. Let's say roughly sixty-two bundles of

five-hundred-euro notes totalling three million ninety-eight thousand euros and seventy-four cents, rounded off to the euro, and equalling six billion old lire.'

'And you believe that?'

'Inspector, I have to believe my client. But the point is not whether I believe him. It's whether the public believes him.'

'But there may be a way to prove that your client is telling the truth.'

'Oh, really? What?'

'Simple. As you yourself said, Mr Peruzzo had very little time to scrape together the ransom money. Therefore there must be bank documents with the related data attesting to the withdrawal of the amount. All you have to do is make these documents public, and your client will have proved his absolute good faith.'

Deep silence.

'Did you hear me, Counsel?'

'Of course. It's the same solution I promptly suggested to him myself.'

'So, as you can see——'

'There's a problem.'

'What?'

'Mr Peruzzo didn't get the money from any banks.'

'Oh, no? Then where did he get it?'

'My client agreed not to reveal the names of those who so generously consented to assist him at this delicate moment. In short, nothing was written down on paper.'

Out of what filthy, stinking sewer had come the hand that gave Peruzzo the money?

'Then the situation seems hopeless to me.'

'To me, too, Inspector. So hopeless, in fact, that I'm beginning to wonder if my counsel is still of any use to Mr Peruzzo.'

So the rats, too, were getting ready to abandon the sinking ship.

✳

The press conference began at five-thirty sharp. Behind a large table sat Minutolo, the judge, the commissioner, and Dr Lattes. The conference hall was packed with journalists, photographers, and cameramen. Nicolò Zito and Pippo Ragonese were there, too, at a proper distance from one another. The first to speak was Commissioner Bonetti-Alderighi, who thought it best to start at the beginning – that is, to explain how the kidnapping came about. He pointed out that this first part of the account was based on declarations made by the girl. On the evening of the abduction, Susanna Mistretta was returning home on her moped, along the road she normally took, when, at the intersection with the San Gerlando trail, right near her house, a car pulled up beside her and forced her to turn onto the unmade road to avoid collision. Upset and confused by the incident, Susanna barely had time to stop before two men got out of the car, their heads covered by ski masks. One of them lifted her bodily and threw her into the car.

Susanna was too stunned to react. The man removed her helmet, pressed a cotton wad to her nose and mouth, gagged her, tied her hands behind her back, and made her lie down at his feet.

In confusion, the girl heard the other man get back in the car, take the wheel, and drive off. At this point she lost consciousness. Investigators hypothesize that the second man had gone to remove the motorbike from the road.

When Susanna woke up, she was in total darkness. She was still gagged, but her hands had been untied. She realized she was in an isolated place. Moving about in the dark, she gathered that she'd been put inside some sort of concrete vat at least ten feet deep. There was an old mattress on the ground. She spent the first night this way, despairing not so much over her own situation, but for her dying mother. Then she must have drifted off to sleep. She woke up when someone turned on a light, a lamp of the sort used by mechanics to light up a car's motor. Two men in ski masks were watching her. One of them took out a small portable cassette recorder, and the other came down into the vat on a ladder. The man with the tape recorder said something while the other removed Susanna's gag. She cried for help, and the gag was put back on. They returned a short while later. One of them came down the same ladder, removed her gag, then climbed back up. The other took a Polaroid snapshot of her. They never gagged her again. To bring her food — always canned — they always used the ladder, which they would lower each time. In one corner of the vat there was a pail for bodily functions. As of that moment the light remained on.

At no time during her confinement was Susanna subjected to any mistreatment. She had no way, however, to attend to her personal hygiene. Nor did she ever hear her abductors speak. And they never once answered her questions or addressed her in any manner. They didn't even say she was about to be freed when they made her come up out of the vat. Later Susanna was able to lead investigators to where she was released. And there, in fact, police found the rope and the handkerchief that had been used to gag her. In conclusion, the commissioner said, the girl was in fairly good condition, considering the terrible ordeal she'd just been through.

Lattes then pointed to a journalist, who stood up and asked why they couldn't interview the girl.

'Because the investigation is still ongoing,' replied the judge.

'In short, was the ransom paid or not?' asked Zito.

'We're not at liberty to reveal that right now,' the judge answered again.

At this point Pippo Ragonese stood up. His lips were pursed so tightly that the words came out compressed.

'I'd like n't t'ask a quest'n b't t'make a st'tm'nt—'

'Speak clearly!' shouted the Greek chorus of journalists.

'I want to make a statement, not to ask a question. Shortly before I came here, our studios received a phone call that was forwarded to me. I recognized the voice of the same kidnapper who had phoned me before. He declared, and I quote, that the ransom had not been paid, and that although the person who was supposed to pay had tricked them, they had decided to set the girl free anyway, because they didn't want to have a death on their conscience.'

Mayhem broke out. People leapt to their feet, gesticulating, other people ran out of the room, the judge inveighed against Ragonese. The uproar got so loud that you couldn't understand a word anyone was saying. Montalbano turned off the television, went out on the veranda, and sat down.

*

Livia got home an hour later and found Salvo looking out at the sea. She didn't seem the least bit angry.

'Where were you?'

'I dropped in to say hi to Beba and then went over to Kolymbetra. Promise me you'll go there one of these days. And where were you? You didn't even phone to say you weren't coming home for lunch.'

'I'm sorry, Livia, but—'

'Don't apologize. I have no desire to quarrel with you. These are our last few hours together, and I don't want to spoil them.'

She flitted about the house a bit, then did something she almost never did. She went and sat on his lap and held him tight. She stayed there awhile, in silence. Then:

'Shall we go inside?' she whispered in his ear.

Before going into the bedroom Montalbano, for one reason or another, unplugged the telephone.

*

As they lay in each other's arms, dinner time passed. And after-dinner time as well.

'I'm so happy Susanna's kidnapping was solved before I left,' Livia said at a certain point.

'Yeah,' replied the inspector.

He'd managed to forget about the abduction for a few hours. But he was instinctively grateful to Livia for having reminded him of it. Why? What did gratitude have to do with it? He had no explanation.

As they ate they spoke little. Livia's imminent departure weighed heavy on both their minds.

She got up from the table and went to finish packing. At some point he heard Livia call from the other room:

'Salvo, did you take the book of yours I was reading?'

'No.'

It was a novel by Simenon, *Monsieur Hire*.

Livia came and sat beside him on the veranda.

'I can't find it. I wanted to take it with me so I can finish it.'

The inspector had a hunch where it might be. He got up.

'Where are you going?'

'I'll be right back.'

The book was where he thought it would be, in the bedroom, caught between the wall and the head of the bed, having fallen off the bedside table. He bent down, picked it up, and put it on top of the already closed suitcase. He went back out on the veranda.

'I found it,' he said, and started to sit back down.

'Where?' asked Livia.

Montalbano froze, thunderstruck. One foot slightly raised, body leaning slightly forward. As if in the throes of a back spasm. He held so still that Livia got scared.

'Salvo, what's wrong?'

He was powerless to move. His legs had turned to lead, but his brain kept whirring, all the gears spinning at high speed, happy to be finally turning the right way.

'My God, Salvo, are you ill?'

'No.'

Ever so slowly, he felt his blood, no longer petrified, begin to flow again. He managed to sit down. But he had an expression of utter astonishment on his face and didn't want Livia to see it.

He rested his head on her shoulder and said:
'Thanks.'

At that moment he understood why, earlier, when they were lying in bed, he'd felt a gratitude for which, at first, he'd had no explanation.

FIFTEEN

When time's mechanism jammed at three twenty-seven and forty seconds, Montalbano didn't wake up, since he was already awake. He hadn't been able to fall asleep. He would have liked to toss and turn in bed, letting himself be carried off by waves of thought following one upon the other like breakers in rough seas, but he was forcing himself not to disturb Livia, who'd fallen asleep almost at once, and therefore he couldn't thrash his arms and legs about.

The alarm went off at six, the weather looked promising, and by seven-fifteen they were already on the road to Punta Raisi, the airport of Palermo. Livia drove. Along the way they spoke little or not at all. Montalbano was already far away, thinking about what he was itching to do, to determine whether the idea he'd had was an absurd fantasy or an equally wild reality. Livia was also lost in thought, worrying about what awaited her in Genoa, the backlog at work, the things left hanging because she'd suddenly needed to go to Vigàta for a long stay at Salvo's side.

Before Livia entered the boarding area, they embraced in the crowd like two teenagers in love. As he held her in his arms, Montalbano felt two conflicting emotions that had no natural right to be together, yet there they were. On the one hand he felt deep sadness that Livia was leaving. Without a doubt the house in Marinella would underscore her absence at every turn, now that he was well on his way to becoming a man of a certain age and starting to feel the weight of solitude. On the other hand he felt rather pressed, anxious for Livia to leave right away, without further delay, so that he could race back to Vigàta to do what he had to do, totally free and no longer obliged to conform to her schedule or answer her questions.

Then Livia broke away, looked back at him, and headed towards the security checkpoint. Montalbano stood still. Not because he wanted to follow her with his eyes until the last moment, but because a kind of astonishment had blocked his next move, which would have been to turn his back and head for the exit. For he thought he'd glimpsed, deep in her eyes — all the way inside — a sort of glimmer, a twinkle that shouldn't have been there. It had lasted barely an instant, then gone out at once, cloaked by the opaque veil of emotion. Yet that flash — muted, yes, but still a flash — had lasted long enough for the inspector to see it and remain bewildered by it. Want to bet that Livia, too, as they were embracing, had felt the same contradictory feelings as he? That she too felt at once bitter over their parting and anxious to get back her freedom?

At first he felt angry, then started laughing. How did the Latin saying go? *Nec tecum nec sine te.* Neither with nor without you. Perfect.

✳

'Montalbano? This is Minutolo.'

'Hi. Were you able to get any useful information out of the girl?'

'That's just it, Montalbà. Part of the problem is that she's still shaken by the abduction, which is logical, and part of it's that she hasn't slept a wink since she's been back, and so she hasn't been able to tell us much.'

'Why hasn't she been able to sleep?'

'Because her mother's taken a turn for the worse and she hasn't wanted to leave her bedside for even a minute. That's why, when I got a call this morning telling me that Signora Mistretta had died during the night—'

'You dashed over there, very tactfully and opportunistically, to interrogate Susanna.'

'I don't do those kinds of things, Montalbà. I came here because I felt it was my duty. After all the time I've spent in this house—'

'You've become like one of the family. Good for you. But I still don't understand why you called me.'

'OK. Since the funeral will be held tomorrow morning, I would like to begin questioning Susanna the day after tomorrow. The judge is in agreement. How about you?'

'What have I got to do with it?'

'Shouldn't you be there too?'

'I don't know. The commissioner will decide whether I should or not. Actually, do me a favour. Give him a ring, see what his orders are, and call me back.'

*

'Is that you, signore? Adelina Cirrinciò here.'

Adelina the housekeeper! How did she already know that Livia was gone? Sense of smell? The wind? Better not to probe too deep. He might discover that everyone in town also knew what tune he hummed when sitting on the toilet.

'What is it, Adelì?'

'Can I come-a this aftanoon to clean house and make you somethin a eat?'

'No, Adelì, not today. Come tomorrow morning.'

He needed a little time to think, alone, with nobody else around.

'D'jou decide yet abou' ma gransson's bappetism?' the housekeeper continued.

He didn't hesitate one second. Thinking she was being clever with her quip about evening things out, Livia had provided him with an excellent reason to accept.

'I've decided, yes, I'll do it.'

'Ah, Gesù, Amma so heppy!'

'Have you set the date?'

'Iss ahp to you, signore.'

'Me?'

'Yes, hit depends on when you free.'

No, it depends on when your son is free, the inspector wanted to say, since Pasquale, the child's father, was always in and out of jail. But he merely said:

'Arrange everything yourselves, then let me know. I've got all the time in the world now.'

*

More than sit down, Francesco Lipari collapsed into the chair in front of the inspector's desk. His face was pale and the circles under his eyes had turned a dense black, as though painted on with shoe polish. His clothes were rumpled, as if he'd slept in them. Montalbano was shocked. He would have expected the boy to be happy and relieved that Susanna had been freed.

'Are you not feeling well?'

'No.'

'Why?'

'Susanna won't speak to me.'

'Explain.'

'What's to explain? Ever since I first heard she'd been released, I've called her house at least ten times. It's always her father, her uncle, or someone else who answers the phone. Never her. And they always tell me Susanna's busy and can't come to the phone. Even this morning, when I heard that her mother had died—'

'Where did you hear it?'

'On a local radio station. I immediately thought: it's a good thing she got to see her again while she was still alive! And so I phoned, I wanted to be near her, but I got the same answer. She wasn't available.'

He buried his face in his hands.

'What did I do to be treated this way?'

'You? Nothing,' said Montalbano. 'But you have to try to understand. The trauma of being kidnapped is tremendous and very hard to get over. Everyone who's been through it says the same thing. It takes time.'

And the Good Samaritan Montalbano fell silent, pleased with himself. All the while he was forming his own, strictly personal opinion of the matter, but preferred not to reveal it to the young man. He therefore stuck to generalities.

'But wouldn't having someone beside her who truly loves her help her to get over the trauma?'

'You want to know something?'

'OK.'

'I'll make a confession. Like Susanna, I think that I, too, would want to be left alone to contemplate my wounds.'

'Wounds?'

'Yes. And not just my own, but those I've inflicted on others.'

The boy looked at him, utterly at sea.

'I have no idea what you're talking about.'

'Never mind.'

The Good Samaritan Montalbano wasn't about to waste his daily dose of goodness all at once.

'Was there anything else you wanted to tell me?' he asked.

'Yes. Did you know that Peruzzo was left off the ballot of his party's candidates?'

'No.'

'And did you know that the Customs Police have been searching his offices since yesterday afternoon? Rumour has it that they found, right off the bat, enough material to put him behind bars.'

'This is the first I've heard of it. And so?'

'So I've been asking myself some questions.'

'And you want me to answer them?'

'If possible.'

'I'm willing to answer one question only, provided I can. Make your choice.'

The boy asked his question at once. Clearly it was the first on his list.

'Do you think it was Peruzzo who put clippings instead of money in that bag?'

'Don't you?'

Francesco attempted a smile, but didn't succeed. He only twisted his mouth into a grimace.

'Don't answer a question with a question,' he said.

He was sharp, this kid. Alert and clever. It was a pleasure to talk to him.

'Why shouldn't I think it was him?' said Montalbano. 'Mr Peruzzo, according to what we've learned about him, is an unscrupulous man with a penchant for dangerous gambits. He probably sized up his situation. The essential thing, for him, was to avoid getting drawn into the case, because once he was, he could only lose. Therefore, why not take yet another risk and try to save six billion lire?'

'And what if they killed Susanna?'

'He could claim, as a last resort, that he'd paid the ransom and that it was the kidnappers who hadn't kept their word. Because there was always the chance that Susanna might recognize one of them, which would have made it necessary to eliminate her. He would have cried and wailed in front of the TV cameras, and some people would have ended up believing him.'

'And would you have been one of those people, Inspector?'

'I really couldn't say,' said Montalbano.

*

'Montalbano? This is Minutolo. I spoke with the commissioner.'

'What'd he say?'

'He said he didn't want to take advantage of your courtesy.'

'Which, translated into the vernacular, means the quicker I get myself out of the way, the better.'

'Precisely.'

'Well, my friend, what do you want me to say? I guess I'll go back to convalescing and wish you all the best.'

'But if I need to exchange a few ideas with you, can I—'

'Whenever you like.'

'Did you know that the Customs Police have found truckloads of incriminating stuff in Peruzzo's offices? Everybody thinks he's screwed for good this time.'

*

He picked up the photographic enlargements that he'd had Cicco De Cicco make and put them in an envelope, which he managed, with some effort, to fit in his jacket pocket.

'Catarella!'

'Your orders, Chief.'

'Is Inspector Augello around?'

'No, Chief. He's in Montelusa 'cause the c'mishner wants 'Specter Augello to be the inner-in-chief.'

So the c'mishner had finally marginalized the inspector and was speaking only to Augello, the inner-in-chief.

'What about Fazio?'

'He ain't here, neither, Chief. He went for a minnit over to Via Palazzolo, 'cross from the alimentary school.'

'What for?'

'There's some shopkeeper who din't wanna pay pertection money shot at the guy who axed him for it but 'e missed.'

'So much the better.'

'Smuch the bitter, Chief, but t'make it up he got some guy who's passin by in the arm.'

'Listen, Cat. I'm going home to resume my convalescence.'

'Straightaway straightaway?'

'Yes.'

'Can I come see you sometimes when I wanna see you sometimes?'

'Come whenever you like.'

*

Before returning to Marinella, he dropped in at the grocer's where he occasionally got his provisions. He bought green olives, *passuluna* black olives, *caciocavallo* cheese, fresh bread sprinkled with *giuggiulena*, and a jar of Trapanese pesto.

Back at home, he set the table on the veranda while the pasta cooked. After shilly-shallying a bit, the day had finally surrendered to the late-spring sunshine. There wasn't a cloud in the sky, not a breath of wind in the air.

The inspector drained the pasta, dressed it with pesto, took the dish outside, and began to eat. A man was walking by along the water, and for a moment he stopped and stared at Montalbano on the veranda. What was so strange about him that a man should eye him as if he were a painting? Perhaps he really was a painting, one that might be titled *The Solitary Pensioner's Lunch*. The idea made him suddenly lose his appetite. He kept eating his pasta, but listlessly.

The telephone rang. It was Livia. She told him she'd made it back without incident, that everything was all right, she was cleaning her apartment, and would call him back that evening. A brief phone call, but long enough to let the pasta turn cold.

He didn't feel like eating any more. A wave of black melancholy had come over him, conceding him only a glass of wine and a bit of *giuggiulena* bread. He tore off a piece, put it in his mouth, and with the index finger of his right hand began searching about for *giuggiulena* seeds that had fallen from the crust. He pressed them against the tablecloth with his fingertip until they stuck, then brought his finger to his mouth. The joy of eating bread with *giuggiulena* lay primarily in this ritual.

Flush against the veranda's right-hand wall — on the outside, that is — was a wild shrub that over time had grown in width and height to the point where it now came up to the level of someone sitting on the bench.

Livia had told him many times that they needed to

uproot it, but this had become a difficult proposition. By now the shrub's roots must have grown as thick and long as a tree's. Montalbano didn't know why, but he suddenly had the urge to cut it down. He needed only to turn his head a little to the right for the whole bush to enter his field of vision. The wild plant was reviving. Here and there amidst its yellow scrub a few green buds were beginning to emerge. Near the top, between two small branches, a silvery spider's web sparkled in the sunlight. Montalbano was certain it hadn't been there the day before, because Livia would have noticed and, with her fear of spiders, would have destroyed it with the broom. It must have been made during the night.

The inspector stood up and leaned over the railing to get a closer look at it.

Spellbound, the inspector counted some thirty threads in concentric circles that decreased in diameter as they approached the centre. The distance between threads was the same throughout, except in the middle, where it greatly increased. The circular weave, moreover, was held together by a regular sequence of radial threads that emanated from the centre and stretched to the outermost circle of the web.

Montalbano guessed that there were about twenty radial threads of uniform distance from one another. The centre of the web was made up of the points of convergence of all the threads, which were held together by a thread different from the rest and spiral in shape.

How patient that spider must have been!

It certainly must have encountered some difficulties. A gust of wind shredding the weave, an animal that happened to pass and move a branch ... But no matter, the spider had carried on its nocturnal labour, determined to bring its web to completion, whatever the cost, obstinate, deaf and blind to all other stimuli.

But where was the spider? Try as he might, the inspector couldn't see it. Had it already left, abandoning everything? Had it been eaten by some other animal? Or was it lurking hidden under a yellow leaf, looking keenly around, with its eight eyes like a diadem, its eight legs ready to spring?

All at once, the web began ever so delicately to vibrate, to quiver. Not from any sudden breath of wind, for the nearest leaves, even the flimsiest, remained still. No, it was an artificial movement, created intentionally. And by what, if not the spider itself? Apparently the invisible arachnid wanted the web to be taken for something else — a veil of frost, a wisp of steam — and was moving the threads with its legs. It was a trap.

Montalbano turned back towards the table, picked up a tiny piece of bread, broke it up into even smaller crumbs, and threw them at the web. Too light, they scattered in the air, but one did get caught in the very middle of the web, right on the spiral thread, and stayed there for only a split-second. It was there one moment and gone the next. Darting out like a flash from the upper part of the web – which remained hidden under some leaves – a grey dot had enveloped the breadcrumb and vanished. But more than actually witness this movement, the inspector had sensed it. The swiftness with which the grey dot had moved was astonishing. He decided he wanted a better look at the spider's reaction. He took another crumb, rolled it into a tiny little ball slightly bigger than the last one, and hurled it right into the centre of the web, which shook all over. The grey dot pounced again, arrived at the centre, covered the bread with its body, but did not return to its hiding place. It held still, perfectly visible, in the middle of its admirable structure of airy geometries. To Montalbano it seemed as if the spider was looking at him, gloating in triumph.

Then, in nightmarishly slow succession, as in an endless cinematic fade-out and fade-in, the spider's tiny head began to change colour and form, going from grey to pink, its fuzz turning to hair, the eight eyes merging into two, until it looked like a minute human face, smiling with satisfaction at the booty it held tightly between its legs.

Montalbano shuddered in horror. Was he living a nightmare? Had he drunk too much wine without realizing it? All at once he remembered a passage in Ovid he'd studied at school, the one about Arachne the weaver, turned into a spider by Athena ... Could time have started running backwards, all the way back to the dark night of myth? He felt dizzy, head spinning. Luckily that monstrous vision didn't last long, for the image began at once to blur and reverse the transformation. Yet before the spider turned back into a spider, before it vanished again amidst the leaves, Montalbano had enough time to recognize the face. And, no, it wasn't Arachne's. He was sure of that.

He sat down on the bench, his legs giving out from under him. He had to drink a whole glass of wine to regain a little strength.

He realized that it must also have been late one night — on one of many nights of anguish, torment, and rage — that the other spider, too, the one whose face he'd just glimpsed, had decided to weave a gigantic web.

And with patience, tenacity, and determination, never once turning back, that spider had woven its web to completion. It was a marvel of geometry, a masterpiece of logic.

Yet it was impossible for that web not to contain at least one mistake, however minuscule, one tiny, barely visible imperfection.

He got up, went inside, and started looking for a magnifying glass that he knew he had somewhere. Ever since Sherlock Holmes, no detective is a true detective if he doesn't have a magnifying glass within reach.

He opened every last drawer in the house, made a mess of the place — coming across a letter he'd received from a friend six months before and never opened, he opened it, read it, learned that his friend Gaspano had become a grandfather (Shit! But weren't he and Gaspano the same age?) — searched some more, then decided there was no point in continuing. He could only conclude, apparently, that he was not a true detective. Elementary, my dear Watson. He went back out on the veranda, leaned on the railing, and bent all the way forward until his nose was almost at the centre of the spider's web. Then he recoiled a little, suddenly scared that the lightning-fast spider might bite his nose, mistaking it for prey. He studied the web carefully, to the point that his eyes began to water. No, the web appeared geometrically perfect, but in reality it wasn't. There were at least three or four points where the distance between one strand and the next was irregular, and there was even one spot where two threads zigzagged for very brief stretches.

Feeling reassured, he smiled. Then his smile turned to laughter. A spider's web! There wasn't a single cliché more used and abused to describe a scheme plotted in the shadows. He'd never employed it before. Apparently the cliché had wanted to get back at him for his disdain, becoming a reality and forcing him to take it into consideration.

SIXTEEN

Two hours later he was in his car on the road to Gallotta, eyes popping because he couldn't remember where he was supposed to turn. At a certain point he spotted, on his right, the tree with the sign saying FRESH EGGS painted in red.

The path from the road led nowhere except to the little white dice of a cottage where he'd been. In fact it ended there. From a distance he noticed a car parked in the space in front of the house. He drove up the path, which was all uphill, parked near the other car, and got out.

The door was locked. Maybe the woman was entertaining a client with other intentions than buying fresh eggs.

He didn't knock, but decided to wait a little. He smoked a cigarette, leaning against his car. As he tossed the butt on the ground, he thought he saw something appear and disappear behind the tiny barred window next to the front door that allowed air to circulate inside when the door was closed. A face, perhaps. The door then opened and a distinguished-looking, chunky man of about fifty came out, wearing gold-rimmed glasses. He was pepper-red with embarrassment.

'Won't you come in, Inspector?' the woman called from inside.

Montalbano went in. She was sitting on the sofa-cot. Its cover was rumpled and a pillow had fallen to the floor. She was buttoning her blouse, long black hair hanging loose on her shoulders, the corners of her mouth smeared with lipstick.

'I looked out the window and recognized you at once,' she said. 'Excuse me just one minute.'

She stood up and started putting things in order. Like the first time he saw her, she was dressed up.

'How is your husband feeling?' Montalbano asked, glancing at the door to the back room, which was closed.

'How's he supposed to feel, poor man?'

When she'd finished tidying up and had wiped her mouth with a Kleenex, she asked with a smile:

'Can I make you some coffee?'

'Thank you. But I don't want to inconvenience you.'

'Are you kidding? You don't seem like a cop. Please sit down,' she said, pulling out a cane chair for him.

'Thanks. I don't know your name.'

'Angela. Angela Di Bartolomeo.'

'Did my colleagues come to interrogate you?'

'Inspector, I did just like you told me to do. I put on shabby clothes, put the bed in the other room ... Nothing doing. They turned the house upside down, they even looked under my husband's bed, they asked me questions for four hours straight, they searched the chicken coop and scared my chickens away and broke three baskets' worth of eggs ... And then there was one of 'em, the son of a bitch — pardon my language — who, as soon as we were alone, took advantage ...'

'Took advantage how?'

'Took advantage of me, touched my breasts. At a certain point it got to where I couldn't take it any more and I started crying. It didn't matter that I kept saying I wouldn't ever do any harm to Dr Mistretta's niece 'cause the doctor even gives my husband his medicines for free ... But he just didn't want to hear it.'

The coffee was excellent.

'Listen, Angela, I need you to try and remember something.'

'I'll do whatever you want.'

'Do you remember when you said that after Susanna was kidnapped, a car came here one night and you thought it might be a client?'

'Yessir.'

'OK, now that things have settled down, can you calmly try to remember what you did when you heard that car's engine?'

'Didn't I already tell you?'

'You said you got out of bed because you thought it was a client.'

'Yessir.'

'A client who hadn't told you he was coming, however.'

'Yessir.'

'You got out of bed, and then what did you do?'

'I came in here and turned on the light.'

This was the new element, the thing the inspector had been looking for. Therefore she must also have seen something, in addition to what she'd heard.

'Stop right there. Which light?'

'The one outside. The one that's over the door and when it's dark it lights up the garden in front of the house. When my husband was still OK, we used to eat outside in the summertime. The switch is right there, see it?'

And she pointed to it. It was on the wall between the door and the little window.

'And then?'

'Then I looked out of the window, which was half open. But the car'd already turned around, I just barely saw it from behind.'

'Do you know anything about cars, Angela?'

'Me?' said the woman. 'I don't know the first thing!'

'But you managed to see the back of the car, you just told me.'

'Yessir.'

'Do you remember what colour it was?'

Angela thought about this for a moment.

'I can't really say, Inspector. Might've been blue, black, dark green ... But I'm sure about one thing: it wasn't light, it was dark.'

Now came the hardest question.

Montalbano took a deep breath and asked it. And Angela answered at once, somewhat surprised at not having thought of it first.

'Oh, yes, that's true!'

Then she immediately made a face, looking confused.

'But ... what's that got to do with it?'

'In fact it's got nothing to do with it,' he hastened to reassure her. 'I asked you because the car I'm looking for looked a lot like that one.'

He got up and held out his hand to her.

'I have to go now.'

Angela also stood up.

'You want a really, really fresh egg?'

Before the inspector could answer, she'd pulled one out of a basket. Montalbano took it, tapped it twice against the table, and sucked out the contents. It had been years since he'd last tasted an egg like that.

*

At a junction on the way back, he saw a sign that said MONTEREALE 18 KM. He turned and took this road.

Perhaps it was the taste of the egg that made him realize he hadn't been to Don Cosimo's shop for quite some time. It was a tiny little place where one could still find things that had long disappeared from Vigàta, such as little bunches of oregano, concentrate of sun-dried tomatoes and, most of all, a special vinegar made from strong, naturally fermented red wine. Indeed he'd noticed that the bottle he had in the kitchen had barely two fingers' worth left. He therefore needed urgently to restock.

It took him an incredibly long time to reach Montereale. He'd driven at a snail's pace, in part because he was thinking of the implications of what Angela had confirmed, in part because he enjoyed taking in the new landscape. In town, as he was about to turn onto the little street that led to the shop, he noticed a sign indicating no entry. This was new. It hadn't been there before. It meant he would have to make a long detour. He was better off leaving the car in the little piazza that was right there, and taking a little walk. He pulled over, stopped, opened the car door, and saw a uniformed traffic policeman in front of him.

'You can't park here.'

'I can't? Why not?'

'Can't you read that sign? No parking.'

The inspector looked around. There were three other vehicles parked in the piazzetta. A small pickup, a mini-van, and a four-by-four.

'What about them?'

The cop looked at him sternly.

'They have authorization.'

Why, nowadays, did every town, even if it had only two hundred inhabitants, pretend it was New York City, passing extremely complicated traffic regulations that changed every two weeks?

'Listen,' the inspector said in a conciliatory tone. 'I only need to stop a few minutes. I want to go to Don Cosimo's shop to buy—'

'You can't.'

'Is it also forbidden to go to Don Cosimo's shop?' said Montalbano, at a loss.

'It's not forbidden,' the traffic cop said. 'It's just that the shop is closed.'

'And when will it reopen?'

'I don't think it will ever open again. Don Cosimo died.'

'Oh my God! When?'

'Are you a relative?'

'No, but . . .'

'Then why are you surprised? Don Cosimo, rest his soul, was ninety-five years old. He died three months ago.'

He drove off cursing the saints. To leave town, he had to take a rather labyrinthine route that ended up setting his nerves on edge. He calmed down when he started driving along the coastal road that led back to

Marinella. All at once he remembered that when Mimì Augello said that Susanna's backpack had been found, he'd specified that they'd found it behind the four-kilometre marker along the road he was on now. He was almost there. He slowed down, pulled over, and stopped at the very point Mimì had mentioned. He got out. There were no houses nearby. To his right were some clumps of wild grass, beyond which lay a golden burst of yellow beach, the same as in Marinella. Beyond that, the sea, surf receding with a lazy breath, already anticipating the sunset. On his left was a high wall, interrupted at one point by a cast-iron gate, which was wide open. At the gate began a paved road that cut straight through a well-tended, genuine wood and led to a villa that remained hidden from view. To one side of the gate was an enormous bronze plaque with letters written in high relief.

Montalbano didn't need to cross the road to read what it said.

He got back in the car and left.

What was it Adelina often said? *L'omu e' sceccu di consiguenza.* Or: Man is a jackass of consequence. A glorified donkey. And like a donkey that always travels the same road and gets used to that road, man is given to taking always the same route, always making the same gestures, without reflection, out of habit.

But would what he had just happened to discover, and what Angela had told him, stand up in court?

No, he concluded, definitely not. But they were confirmations. That, they certainly were.

*

At seven thirty he turned on the television to watch the evening's first news report.

They said there were no new developments in the investigation. Susanna was still unable to answer questions, and a huge crowd was expected at the funeral services for the late Mrs Mistretta, despite the fact that the family had made it known they didn't want anyone to come either to the church or the cemetery. They also mentioned in passing that Antonio Peruzzo had vanished from circulation, fleeing his impending arrest. This news, however, had not been officially confirmed. The other station's news broadcast, at eight, repeated the same things, but in a different order. First came the report of the engineer's disappearance, then the fact that the family wanted a private funeral. Nobody could enter the church, and no one would be allowed into the cemetery.

*

The telephone rang, just as he was about to go out to eat. He had a hearty appetite. He'd eaten hardly anything at midday, and Angela's fresh egg had tasted to him like an hors d'oeuvre.

'Inspector? This ... this is Francesco.'

251

He didn't recognize the voice. It was hoarse, hesitant.

'Francesco who?' he asked gruffly.

'Francesco Li ... Lipari.'

Susanna's boyfriend. Why was he talking like that?

'What's wrong?'

'Susanna...'

He stopped. Montalbano could clearly hear him snif-
fle. The kid was crying.

'Susanna ... Susanna told ... me ...'

'Did you see her?'

'No. But she ... she finally ... answered the phone...'

Now came the sobbing.

'I'm ... I'm ... sorr...'

'Calm down, Francesco. Do you want to come over to
my place?'

'No ... no thanks ... I'm not ... I've been drin ...
drinking. She said she didn't want to ... to see me any
more.'

Montalbano felt his blood run cold, perhaps colder
than Francesco's. What did this mean? That Susanna had
another man? And if she had another man, then all his
calculations, all his suppositions went out the window.
They were nothing more than the ridiculous, miserable
fantasies of an ageing inspector who was no longer all
there in the head.

'Is she in love with somebody else?'

'Worse.'

'Worse in what way?'

'There isn't anybo ... anybody else. She made a vow, a decision, when she was being held prisoner.'

'Is she religious?'

'No. It's a promise she made to herself ... that if she was set free in time to see her mother still alive ... she would go away before a month had passed. And she was talking to me as though she was already gone, already far away.'

'Did she tell you where she was going?'

'To Africa. She's giving up her studies, giving up getting married, having children. Sh-she's giving up everything.'

'To do what?'

'To make herself useful. That's exactly what she said: "I'm finally going to make myself useful." She's going away with some volunteer organization. And you know what? She'd already made her preliminary request with them two months ago, without telling me anything. All the while she was with me, she was thinking of leaving me forever. What on earth got into her?'

So there wasn't any other man. And it all made sense. Even more than before.

'Do you think she may change her mind?'

'No, Inspector. If you'd heard her voice ... And anyway, I know her well. When she's made a de-decision ... But for the love of God, what does it mean, Inspector? What does it mean?'

The last question was a cry. Montalbano knew perfectly

well, at this point, what it meant, but he couldn't answer Francesco's question. For the inspector it had all become rather simple. The scales, which had long been in a state of balance, had now tipped forcefully and entirely to one side. What Francesco had just told him confirmed that his next move was the right one. And should be made at once.

*

Before making any moves, however, he had to fill Livia in. He put his hand over the telephone, but did not pick up the receiver. He still needed to talk it over with himself. Did what he was about to do, he asked himself, in some way mean that, having reached the end of his career, or almost, he was repudiating – in the eyes of his superiors, in the eyes of the law itself – the principles by which he had abided for so many long years? But had he in fact *always* respected these principles? Didn't Livia harshly accuse him once of acting like a minor god, a little god who took pleasure in changing or rearranging the facts? Livia was wrong. He was no god. Absolutely not. He was only a man with his own personal judgement of right and wrong. And sometimes what he thought was right would have been wrong in the eyes of justice. And vice versa. So was it better to act in accordance with justice, the kind of justice that's written down in books, or with one's own conscience?

No, Livia might not understand, and might even

manage, through argument, to bring him to the opposite
conclusion from the one he wanted to arrive at.

It was better to write to her. He took out a sheet of
paper and a ballpoint pen.

Livia my love,

he began, but couldn't continue. He tore up the sheet
and took out another.

My beloved Livia,

and he got stuck again. He took out a third sheet.

Livia,

and the pen refused to go any further.

It was hopeless. He would tell her everything face to
face, looking her straight in the eye, the next time they
saw each other.

Having made this decision, he felt rested, serene,
revived. *Wait a minute,* he said to himself. *Those three adjectives,
rested, serene, revived, are not your own. You're quoting. OK,
but what?* He thought hard, putting his head in his hands.
Then, confident in his visual memory, he moved with
near-total assurance. He stood up right in front of the
bookcase, pulled out Leonardo Sciascia's *Council of Egypt,*
and leafed through it. There it was, on page 122 of the
first edition from 1966, the one he'd read at age sixteen
and had always carried around with him, to read from
time to time.

On that extraordinary page, the abbé Vella decides
to reveal something to Monsignor Airoldi that will turn
his life upside down, to wit, that the Arabian Code is an

imposture, a forgery created by his own hand. Yet before going to Monsignor Airoldi, the abbé Vella takes a bath and drinks a coffee.

Montalbano, too, stood at a crossroads.

Smiling, he stripped naked and slipped into the shower. He changed all his clothes, down to his underpants, putting on an entire set of clean articles. He chose a serious-looking tie for the occasion. Then he made coffee and drank a cup with relish. By this point, the three adjectives, *rested, serene, revived*, were entirely his. One, however — which was not in Sciascia's book — was missing: *sated*.

*

'What can I get for you, Inspector?'

'Everything.'

They laughed.

Seafood antipasto, fish soup, boiled octopus dressed with olive oil and lemon, four mullets (two fried, two grilled), and two little glasses, filled to the brim, of a tangerine liqueur with an explosive alcohol level, the pride and joy of Enzo the restaurateur. Who congratulated the inspector.

'I can see you're in good form again.'

'Thanks. Would you do me a favour, Enzo? Could you look up Dr Mistretta's number in the phone book and write it down for me on a piece of paper?'

As Enzo was working for him, he drank a third glass of liqueur at his leisure. The restaurateur returned and handed him the number.

'People around town have been talking about the doctor,' he said.

'And what are they saying?'

'That this morning he went to the notary's to do the paperwork for donating the villa he lives in. He's going to move in with his brother, the geologist, now that his wife has passed away.'

'Who's he donating the villa to?'

'Oh, apparently some orphanage in Montelusa.'

From the restaurant phone, Montalbano called first Dr Mistretta's office, then his home. There was no answer. No doubt the doctor was at his brother's villa for the wake. And no doubt only the family was there, unbothered by policemen or journalists. He dialled the number. The telephone rang a long time before somebody picked up.

'The Mistretta home.'

'Montalbano here. Is that you, Doctor?'

'Yes.'

'I need to talk to you.'

'Look, we can do it tomorrow after—'

'No.'

The doctor's voice cracked.

'You want to see me now?'

'Yes.'

The doctor let a little time elapse before speaking again.

'All right, though I find your insistence quite inappropriate. You're aware that the funeral is tomorrow?'

'Yes.'

'Will it take very long?'

'I can't say.'

'Where do you want to meet?'

'I'll be over in twenty minutes, maximum.'

Exiting the trattoria, he noticed that the weather had changed. Heavy rain clouds were approaching from the sea.

SEVENTEEN

Seen from the outside, the villa was in total darkness, a black bulk against a sky black with night and clouds. Dr Mistretta had opened the gate and stood there waiting for the inspector's car to appear. Montalbano drove in, parked, and got out, but waited in the garden for the doctor to close the gate. A faint light shone from a lone window with its shutter ajar; it came from the dead woman's room, where her husband and daughter were keeping watch. One of the two French doors in the salon was closed, the other ajar, but it cast only a dim light into the garden, because the overhead chandelier was not lit.

'Come inside.'

'I prefer to stay outside. We can go in if it starts raining,' said the inspector.

They walked in silence to the wooden benches and sat down like the time before. Montalbano pulled out a packet of cigarettes.

'Want one?'

'No, thank you. I've decided to give up smoking.'

Apparently the kidnapping had led both uncle and niece to make vows.

'What was it you so urgently needed to tell me?'

'Where are your brother and Susanna?'

'In my sister-in-law's room.'

Who knows whether they'd opened the window to let a little air into the room? Who knows whether there was still that ghastly, unbearable stench of medication and illness?

'Do they know I'm here?'

'I told Susanna, but not my brother.'

How many things had been kept, and were still being kept, from the poor geologist?

'So, what did you want to tell me?'

'Let me preface it by saying that I'm not here in an official capacity. But I can be if I want.'

'I don't understand.'

'You will. It depends on your answers.'

'Then get on with your questions.'

That was the problem. The first question was like a first step down a path of no return. He closed his eyes – the doctor couldn't see, anyway – and began.

'You have a patient who lives in a cottage off the road to Gallotta, a man who flipped his tractor and—'

'Yes.'

'Do you know the Good Shepherd Clinic, which is two and a half miles from—'

'What kind of questions are these? Of course I know it. I go there often. So what? Are you going to recite a list of my patients?'

No. No list of patients. L'omu è sceccu di consiguenza. And you, that night in your four-by-four, with your heart racing madly, your blood pressure soaring because of what you were doing — since you had to deposit the helmet and backpack in two different places — what roads did you take? The ones you knew best! It was almost as though you weren't driving the car, but it was driving you . . .

'I just wanted to point out to you that Susanna's helmet was found near the path leading to your patient's house, and the backpack was recovered almost directly in front of the Good Shepherd Clinic. Did you know?'

'Yes.'

Matre santa! Bad move! The inspector would never have expected it.

'And how did you find out?'

'From newspapers, the television, I don't remember.'

'Impossible. The newspapers and television never mentioned those discoveries. We succeeded in letting nothing leak out.'

'Wait! Now I remember! You told me yourself, when we were sitting right here, on this very bench!'

'No, Doctor. I told you those objects had been found, but I didn't say where. And you know why? Because you didn't ask me.'

And that was the snag which at the time the inspector

had perceived as a kind of hesitation and couldn't immediately explain. It was a perfectly natural question, but
it hadn't been asked, and actually stopped the flow of the
discussion, like a line omitted from a printed page. Even
Livia had asked him where he'd found the Simenon novel!
And the oversight was due to the fact that the doctor
knew perfectly well where the helmet and backpack had
been found.

'But ... but, Inspector! There could be dozens of
possible explanations for why I didn't ask you! Do you
realize what kind of state I was in at the time? You want
to construct God knows what out of the flimsiest of—'

'The flimsiest of spider's webs, perhaps? You have
no idea how apt the metaphor is. Just think, initially my
construction rested on an even flimsier thread.'

'Well, if you're the first to admit it . . .'

'Indeed I am. And it concerned your niece. Something
Francesco, her ex-boyfriend, said to me. Do you know
Susanna has left him?'

'Yes, she's already told me about it.'

'It's a touchy subject. I'm a bit reluctant to broach it,
but—'

'But you have to do your job.'

'Do you think I would act this way if I was doing my
job? What I was going to say was: But I want to know
the truth.'

The doctor said nothing.

At that moment a female figure appeared on the

threshold of the French window, took a step forward, and stopped.

Jesus, the nightmare was coming back! It was a bodiless head, with long blonde hair, suspended in air! Just as he'd seen at the centre of the spider's web! Then he realized that Susanna was wearing all black, to mourn her mother, and her clothes blended in with the night.

The girl resumed walking, came towards them, and sat down on a bench. As the light didn't reach that far, one could only barely make out her hair, a slightly less dense point of darkness. She didn't greet them. Montalbano decided to continue as though she wasn't there.

'As often happens between lovers, Susanna and Francesco had intimate relations.'

The doctor became agitated, uneasy.

'You have no right ... And anyway, what's that got to do with your investigation?' he said with irritation.

'It's got a lot to do with it. You see, Francesco told me he was always the one to ask, if you know what I mean. Whereas, on the day she was kidnapped, it was she who took the initiative.'

'Inspector, honestly, I do not understand what my niece's sexual behaviour has to do with any of this. And I wonder if you know what you're saying or are simply raving. So I'll ask you again, what is the point?'

'The point is that when Francesco told me this, he said Susanna may have had a premonition ... But I don't believe in premonitions. It was something else.'

'And what, in your opinion, was it?' the doctor asked sarcastically.

'A farewell.'

What had Livia said the evening before her departure? 'These are our last hours together, and I don't want to spoil them.' She'd wanted to make love. And to think that theirs was to be only a brief separation. What if it had been a long and final goodbye? Because Susanna was already thinking that regardless of whether her plans came to a good or bad end, they inevitably spelled the end of their love. This was the price, the infinitely high price, that she had to pay.

'Because she'd put in her request to go to Africa two months before,' the inspector continued. 'Two months. Which was surely when she got that other idea.'

'What other idea? Listen, Inspector, don't you think you're abusing—'

'I'm warning you,' Montalbano said icily. 'You're giving the wrong answers and asking the wrong questions. I came here to lay my cards on the table and reveal my suspicions . . . or rather, my hopes.'

Why had he said 'hopes'? Because hope was what had tipped the scales entirely to one side, in Susanna's favour. Because that word was what had finally convinced him.

The word completely flummoxed the doctor, who wasn't able to say anything. And for the first time, out of the silence and darkness came the girl's voice, a hesitant voice, as though laden, indeed, with hope: the hope of being understood, to the bottom of her heart.

'Did you say . . . hope?'

'Yes. The hope that a great capacity for hatred might turn into a great capacity for love.'

From the bench where the girl was sitting he heard a kind of sob, which was immediately stifled. He lit a cigarette and saw, by the lighter's glow, that his hand was trembling slightly.

'Want one?' he asked the doctor.

'I said no.'

They were firm in their resolutions, these Mistrettas. So much the better.

'I know there was no kidnapping. That evening, you, Susanna, took a different road home, a little-used unmade road, where your uncle was waiting for you in his four-by-four. You left your motorbike there, got in the car, and crouched down in the back. And your uncle drove off to his villa. There, in the building next to the doctor's villa, everything had been prepared some time before: a bed, provisions, and so on. The cleaning woman had no reason whatsoever to set foot in there. Who would ever have thought of looking for the kidnap victim at her uncle's house? And that was where you recorded the messages. Among other things, you, Doctor, in your disguised voice, spoke of billions. It's hard for people over a certain age to get used to thinking in euros. That was also where you shot your Polaroids, on the back of which you wrote some words, trying your best to make your handwriting legible, since, like all doctors' handwriting, yours is indecipherable. I've never been inside that building, Doctor, but I can say for certain that you had a new telephone extension installed—'

'How can you say that?' asked Carlo Mistretta.

'I know because the two of you came up with a truly brilliant idea for averting suspicion. You seized an opportunity on the fly. After learning that I was coming to the villa, Susanna called in the second recorded message, the one specifying the ransom amount, as I was speaking with you. But I heard, without understanding at first, the sound a phone makes when the receiver on an extension is picked up. Anyway, it wouldn't be hard to get confirmation. All I need to do is call the phone company. And that could constitute evidence, Doctor. Shall I go on?'

'Yes.'

It was Susanna who'd answered.

'I also know, because you told me yourself, Doctor, that there is an old winepress in that building. Thus there must be an adjacent space with the vat for the fermentation of the must. I am willing to bet that this room has a window. Which you, Doctor, opened when you took the snapshot, since it was daytime. You also used a mechanic's lamp to better illuminate the inside of the vat. But there's one detail you neglected in this otherwise elaborate, convincing production.'

'A detail?'

'Yes, Doctor. In the photograph, right below the edge of the vat, there's what appears to be a crack. I had that detail enlarged. It's not a crack.'

'What is it?'

The inspector could feel that Susanna had been about to ask the same question. They still couldn't figure out where they'd made a mistake. He sensed the motion of the doctor's head as it turned toward Susanna, the questioning look in his eyes, even though these things were not visible.

'It's an old fermentation thermometer. Unrecognizable, covered with spider's webs, blackened, and so encrusted into the wall that it looks like it's part of it. And therefore you couldn't see it. But it's still there. And this is the conclusive proof. I need only get up, go inside, pick up the phone, have two of my men come and stand guard over you, call the judge for the warrant, and begin searching your villa, Doctor.'

'It would be a big step forward for your career,' Mistretta said mockingly.

'Once again, you're entirely wrong. My career has no more steps to take, neither forward nor backward. What I'm trying to do is not for you, Doctor.'

'Are you doing it for me?'

Susanna sounded astonished.

Yes, for you. Because I've been spellbound by the quality, the intensity, the purity of your hatred. I am fascinated by the fiendish nature of the thoughts that come into your head, by the coldness and courage and patience with which you carried out your intentions, by the way you calculated the price you had to pay and were ready to pay it. And I'm also doing it for myself, because it's not right that there's always someone who suffers and someone who benefits from the other's suffering, with the approval of the so-called law. Can a man, having reached the end of his career, rebel against a state of things he himself has helped to maintain?

Since the inspector wasn't answering, the girl said something that wasn't even a question.

'The nurse told me you wanted to see Mama.'

I wanted to see her, yes. To see her in bed, wasted away, no longer a body but almost a thing, yet something that groaned, that suffered horribly ... Though I didn't realize it at the time, I wanted to see where your hatred had first taken root and grown uncontrollably with the stench of medications, excrement, sweat, sickness, vomit, pus, and gangrene that had devastated the heart of that thing lying in bed. The hatred with which you infected those close to you ... But not your father — no, your father never knew a thing, never knew that it was all a sham ... He anguished terribly over what he believed was a real kidnapping ... But this, too, was a price you were willing to pay, and to have others pay, because true hatred, like love, doesn't baulk at the despair and tears of the innocent.

'I wanted to understand.'

It began to thunder out at sea. The lightning was far away, but the rain was approaching.

'Because the idea of taking revenge on your uncle was first born in that room, on one of those terrible nights you spent taking care of your mother. Isn't that so, Susanna? At first it seemed like an effect of your fatigue, your discouragement, your despair, but soon it became harder and harder to get that idea out of your head. And so, almost as a way to kill time, you started thinking of how you might make your obsession a reality. You drew up a plan, night after night. And you asked your uncle to help you, because...'

Stop. You can't say that. It just came to you now, this very moment. You need to think it over before—

'Say it,' the doctor said softly but firmly. 'Because Susanna realized that I had always been in love with Giulia. It was a love without hope, but it prevented me from having a life of my own.'

'And therefore you, Doctor, on impulse, you decided to collaborate on the destruction of Antonio Peruzzo's reputation. By manipulating public opinion to perfection. The coup de grâce came when you replaced the money-filled suitcase with the duffel bag full of scrap paper.'

It began to drizzle. Montalbano stood up.

'Before leaving, to set my conscience at rest...'

His voice came out too solemnly, but he was unable to change it.

'To set my conscience at rest, I cannot allow those six billion lire to remain in—'

'In our hands?' Susanna finished his sentence. 'The money is no longer here. We didn't even keep the money that was lent by Mama and never given back. Uncle Carlo took care of it, with the help of a client of his, who will never talk. It was divided up, and by now most of it has already been transferred abroad. It's supposed to be sent anonymously to about fifty different humanitarian organizations. If you want, I can go in the house and get the list.'

'Fine,' said the inspector. 'I'm leaving.'

He indistinctly saw the doctor and the girl stand up as well.

'Are you coming to the funeral tomorrow?' asked Susanna. 'I would really like—'

'No,' said the inspector. 'My only wish is that you, Susanna, do not betray my hope.'

He realized he was talking like an old man, but this time he didn't give a damn.

'Good luck,' he said in a soft voice.

He turned his back to them, went out to his car, opened the door, turned on the ignition, and drove, but had to stop almost at once in front of the closed gate. He saw the girl come running under the now driving rain, her hair seeming to light up like fire when caught in the glare of the headlights. She opened the gate without turning around to look at him. And he, too, looked away.

✻

On the road back to Marinella, the rain started falling in buckets. At a certain point he had to pull over because the windscreen wipers couldn't handle it. Then it stopped all at once. Entering the dining room, he realized he'd left the French door to the veranda open, and the floor had got all wet. He would have to mop it up. He turned on the outdoor light and went outside. The violent rainstorm had washed away the spider's web. The shrub's branches were sparkling clean and dripping wet.

Author's Note

This story is invented from top to bottom, at least I hope it is.

Therefore the names of the characters and business, and the situations and events of the book, have no connection to reality.

If anyone should find some reference to real events, I can assure you this was not intentional.

A. C.

Notes

page 8 – **he couldn't bring himself to go and see the notary** – In Italy a notary *(notaio)* performs functions of probate and contract law, among other things.

page 9 – *'The poor man, not knowing how much he'd bled, / kept on fighting when in fact he was dead.'* – *Il pover'uom, che non se n'era accorto, /* *andava combattendo ed era morto.* Two lines from a traditional Italian song.

page 19 – *a triumphant member of the party in power* – i.e., the party called Forza Italia, the right-wing political entity created by media tycoon Silvio Berlusconi, who was still in power when this book was written.

page 23 – **'Go and see if it was the traffic police!'** – In Italy the jurisdiction of the Vigili Urbani (the 'municipal police'), which includes the traffic police, is separate from that of the Commissariato di Pubblico Sicurezza ('Commissariat of Public Safety'), the branch of the police for which Montalbano works. The Carabinieri (the national police), the Guardia di Finanza (here translated as 'customs police'), and the Polizia Stradale

275

(or 'road police') also have separate jurisdictions, which often leads to petty rivalries and bureaucratic confusion.

page 38 – *'Matre santa!'* – Holy mother! A Sicilian invocation of the Blessed Virgin.

page 44 – **'will be handled by Inspector Minutolo, who, being a Calabrian...'** – What? **Minutolo was from Alì, in Messina province** – Messina is in Sicily, not Calabria. The region of Calabria, across the Strait of Messina from Sicily, is notorious for its kidnappings.

page 45 – **'that would make him the Po, whereas I would be the Dora, the Riparia or the Baltea...'** – The Po is a major river in the north of Italy, of which the Dora, Riparia, and Baltea are tributaries.

page 45 – **the Valley of the Temples** – Probably the finest group of Ancient Greek ruins in Sicily (and there are many), the Valley of the Temples is just outside of Agrigento, the city on which the fictional Montelusa is based.

page 46 – *The number you have reached does not exist* – The recorded response for non-working numbers in Italy indeed says, '*Il numero selezionato da lei è inesistente.*'

page 72 – *'cornuto'* – Italian for 'cuckold', *cornuto* is a common insult throughout the country, but a special favourite among southerners, Sicilians in particular.

page 91 – **the private television station where Nicolò Zito worked** – In Italy there are three state-owned television stations, Rai Uno, Rai Due, Rai Tre and their local subsidiaries, and countless private stations.

page 96 – *a cacocciola* – Sicilian expression used to denote the interrogative gesture, common throughout Italy, where one holds the hand palm-up, fingertips and thumb gathered together and pointing upward, and shakes it lightly. *Cacocciola* is Sicilian for 'artichoke' (*carciofo* in Italian).

page 99 – 'Totò and Peppino' – Totò was the stage and screen name of Antonio de Curtis (1898–1967), perhaps the most celebrated comic actor of the twentieth century in Italy. Also a poet and writer of Neapolitan songs, he was born a marquis and later granted a whole series of noble titles, including Count Palatine, Exarch of Ravenna, Duke of Macedonia and Illyria, and Prince of Constantinople. He was known affectionately as the Principe della Risata, or the Prince of Laughter. Peppino de Filippo (1903–1980) was a Naples-born comic actor of the screen and stage and brother of comic playwright and actor Eduardo de Filippo. He teamed up with Totò in the early 1950s on a series of madcap comic films that became wildly popular.

page 106 – spaghetti *all'aglio e olio* – That is, with 'garlic and oil', and usually a bit of hot pepper and parsley. Because it's considered a light dish, *spaghetti all'aglio e olio* is often served to people who aren't feeling well.

page 107 – aiole – *Aiola* is the Sicilian name for a kind of sea bream (*Pagellus mormyrus* or *Lithognathus mormyrus*) common to Sicilian waters. In Italian it's called *mormora*.

page 115 – '*Madonna biniditta!*' – Blessed Virgin! (Sicilian dialect).

page 120 – 'he's liable to have us searching all the way to the Aspromonte.' – The Aspromonte (literally, 'harsh mountain') is in Calabria, the last stretch of the so-called Calabrian Alps, which are a continuation of the Apennine chain that runs down the Italian peninsula. Augello's quip is predicated on the commissioner's confusion of parts of Sicily with Calabria (see note to page 44).

page 131 – 'that class of shopkeepers who think a thousand lire's the same as a euro' – To the great dismay of many consumers, when the Italian currency was changed from the lira to the euro in 2002, many shops, restaurants, and other small businesses began charging a whole euro for what had previously cost one thousand lire, which in fact was equivalent to barely more than half a euro. Thus a hotel room that had previously cost 100,000 lire (about £35) now cost 100 euros (about £67, at the time of the conversion), and a plate of pasta that had been 12,000 (about £4) suddenly went for 12 euros (£8). By merely moving the decimal point over three places on their prices, many businesses ended up charging their customers twice as much as before. Six billion lire in 2004 was a little over three million euros, or two million pounds.

page 137 – "Operation Clean Hands" – 'Clean Hands' is English for Mani Pulite, the name given by journalists to a nationwide judicial and police investigation in the early 1990s that exposed the endemic corruption of the Italian political system as well as the vast web of collusion between certain politicians, business leaders, intelligence organizations, organized crime, and extremist right-wing groups. After a rash of indictments of political and business leaders, and even a few suicides, Mani Pulite ultimately led to the demise and dissolution of the Christian Democratic Party, which had governed Italy since the end of the Second World War. The Italian Socialist and Social Democratic parties were also dissolved before being reconstituted in other political formations. Unfortunately many of the legal reforms instituted during Mani Pulite have since been reversed under the rule of Silvio Berlusconi's Forza Italia Party.

page 141 – 'Then, with the new law, he brought it back in, paid his percentage, and put his affairs in order' – Former Prime Minister Silvio Berlusconi's ruling party passed a law that allowed money that had been illegally taken out of the country to be repatriated upon payment of a relatively light fine. The law amounted to an amnesty for the sort of corrupt activities that Mani Pulite had attempted to eradicate.

page 149 – It was as if the inspector had spoken to crows – The Sicilian expression *parlare con le ciaùle* (or *ciavule*), i.e., 'to speak to crows', means to be privy to information unknown to most people. *Ciaùla* (or *ciavula*) can also refer to a very talkative woman.

page 159 – since Peruzzo was a victim of the communist judiciary – In attempting to discredit the many judicial inquiries into his and others' corrupt business dealings and the conflicts of interest between their private holdings and their public offices, (former) Prime Minister Berlusconi has repeatedly and speciously claimed that the magistrates behind these investigations are motivated not by any desire to enforce the law but by communist ideology and sympathies, which would make them the natural enemies of the free-enterprise system of which Il Cavaliere presents himself as the champion. Thus any similar investigation into shady financial manoeuvres such as Peruzzo's must have the same motivations behind it.

page 170 – Except that here the odour was denser. [...] It was, moreover, brownish-yellow in colour, with streaks of fiery red. – As seen in many of the earlier novels in this series, Montalbano has a synaesthetic sense of smell, whereby he perceives odours as colours.

page 198 – 'says he's the moon' – *Luna* means 'moon' in Italian.

page 198 – '*Pay them no mind, but look and move on,* as the poet says.' – Mr Luna is making the same mistake as many other Italians in attributing this line – '*Non ti curar di lor, ma guarda e passa*' – to Dante ('the poet'). In fact it is from the Emilio De Marchi translation of La Fontaine's *Fables* (in the story of 'The Lion, the Monkey, and Two Donkeys'). It must be said, however, that in translating in this fashion the line '*mais laissons là ces gens*' (which simply means 'but let us leave those people there'), De Marchi (1851–1901) was purposely echoing Dante's line (*Inferno* 3, l. 51), '*Ma non ragionam di lor, ma guarda e passa*' ('Let us talk not of them, but look and move on').

page 200 – *L'Osservatore Romano* – The official daily newspaper of the Vatican.

page 201 – *Junior Woodchucks' Guidebook* – The Junior Wood-chucks is a Scout organization in the fictional town of Duckburg, the setting for the Donald Duck comic-book and cartoon stories. Donald's nephews Huey, Dewey, and Louie are all Junior Woodchucks, and Scrooge McDuck provides the financial support for the organization. *The Junior Woodchucks' Guidebook* is the all-important manual that tells them how to proceed in certain difficult situations, such as pulling people out of quicksand, crossing a river full of crocodiles, or using pepper to make dragons sneeze. Only Junior Woodchucks are allowed to use the *Guidebook*, though an exception is made for Scrooge.

page 204 – a kind of *autostrada* – The *autostrada* (like the German *autobahn* and the French *autoroute*) is a high-speed superhighway.

page 204 – **ninety miles an hour** – The Berlusconi government indeed raised the maximum speed on the *autostrada* to 150 kph, roughly 90 mph.

page 214 – *cavatuna* [...] **caponata** – *Cavatuna* are a kind of handmade pasta crushed with a fork or one's thumb against a grater, so they remain scored on the outside. The crushing makes them concave or hollow on one side, hence the name (*cavato* means 'hollow' or 'carved out'). *Caponata* is a kind of ratatouille of aubergine, tomato, green pepper, garlic, onion, celery, black olives, vinegar, olive oil, and anchovies. It is sometimes served as a side dish, sometimes as a main course, and here serves as the base for *coniglio all'agrodolce*.

page 236 – *giuggiulena* – Sicilian for sesame.

page 236 – **Trapanese pesto** – *Pesto alla trapanese*, like its cousin, *pesto alla genovese*, is a sauce for pasta with ground or finely chopped basil as its foundation. The Trapanese version (from the Sicilian city of Trapani), however, uses finely chopped and toasted blanched almonds instead of pine nuts, as well as several finely chopped, uncooked tomatoes, which are ground into the blend with garlic, olive oil, and black pepper. Finally, after it is served on the pasta one adds a sprinkling of toasted breadcrumbs in the place of cheese.

page 266 – **'But I heard, without understanding at first, the sound a phone makes when a receiver on an extension is picked up.'** – In Italy, a phone will give an ever so slight ring when the receiver on an extension is either picked up or hung up.

Notes by Stephen Sartarelli